THE SANCTUARY

THE
SANCTUARY

GUSTAVO EDUARDO ABREVAYA

Translated by Andrea G. Labinger

SCHAFFNER PRESS
TUCSON, ARIZONA

First English Language Edition

Trade Paperback Original

Cover & Interior design by Evan Johnston

Library of Congress Control Number: 2023937494

ISBN: 978-1-63964-022-5 (Paperback)

ISBN: 978-1-63964-023-2 (EPUB)

ISBN: 978-1-63964-043-0 (EPDF)

Printed in the United States

To my wife, always

Lacrimosa dies illa,
qua resurget ex favila
iudicandus homo reus.
REQUIEM MASS

{ I }
INTROITUS

"THE CAMERA PANS slowly, from right to left and back again," Álvaro explained, standing in the middle of the road with the camera mounted on his shoulder, filming takes. "The entire, empty expanse of road stretches out before you, desert on both sides, and a brutal sun that falls like lead, accompanied by the lighting, which is sheer and bright, forming a stark contrast with the interior shots, à la John Ford, *Stagecoach*, let's say, or like some Peckinpah productions, essentially *The Wild Bunch*, you know what I mean? That familiar steam rises from the asphalt and blurs the images, as you know, and gives them that shimmer as if they were moving, it's a pretty classic optical effect, and on the horizon a sort of pond seems to form, as unreal as a mirage. Do you see it, Alicia? As a title, maybe *Mirage*? Or *Steam and Sand*? It's nearly midday, and Álvaro and Alicia— because that's what we're going to call them, like us—it's our adventure, remember; you could even be the lead and play the role of Alicia, and of course I'd be Álvaro, it's my way of immortalizing us—are standing in the middle of nothingness, a place not quite as arid as the Sahara in *Lawrence of Arabia*, to give you a sense of it, waiting for a car to come along and rescue them. That's where the idea of emptiness comes into play: devoid of people, of help, of plans. We're talking about the precariousness of life; that has to be implicit, but also made very clear. When emptiness is the only presence, it produces vertigo—how do you like that? Can you see it?" Álvaro asked Alicia, fascinated by the contrast of some rustic herbs growing alongside the road. "*The Presence of Emptiness*, it's very paradoxical and full of fleeting beauty, a fatal oxymoron, opposites playing with the destiny of a man who doesn't accept the rules. The title sounds like something by Bergman. Now, the camera makes a one hundred and eighty-degree turn and you can see the car, a red Chevy coupe, Seventy-six model, a beauty, resting on the sand, two wheels on the road, the coupe tragically listing to the right, its hood raised and the motor steaming. This needs to be very painful for the viewer; it's an esthetic pain, even more painful considering the hero's indifference toward his prized vehicle. He doesn't love it, but he needs it—pay attention here—it's a pact you see every day. Oh yeah, I really like this. Ry Cooder plays in the background, yeah, like in *Paris, Texas*—I love this. Even though it's more like David Lynch, who also has his empty roads, let me remind you. Now our hero, Álvaro, walks along, back and forth, heavy footsteps, revealing his somber mood; the guy's really annoyed, but he's got it all together, evaluating the situation: how much time they have left, possible outcomes, solutions, especially solutions, and he identifies them quickly, because he knows it's a matter of mental agility. This is what he does while Alicia—what could that Jean Harlow-style bleached blonde possibly be doing? If she ever stopped dyeing her hair, she'd look just like you, darling, a curly-haired brunette, my type…" Álvaro went on, smacking his lips and gazing into Alicia's eyes, as black as her curls: "But meantime, come on and show me how clever you are and how self-critical: What could she be doing, with that platinum blonde hair of hers? Of course: sunbathing. She's leaning against the car, with her standard-issue Marilyn sunglasses, you know the ones I mean: they're like a black mask with silver decorations at the tips, quite classic. She's got a kerchief wrapped around her head, super-tight, red Capri pants, an embroidered white blouse tied at the hip so you can see her navel—a very important detail—and on her feet, little black flats, of course. The chick's an icon. Álvaro is the perfect complement, the yang to her yin, hard and distant, badly shaved, a tough-guy profile with a cigarette butt dangling from his mouth. His mirrored Ray-Bans reflect the deadly horizon as he stands there with the slight trace of a smile. Naturally, he wears his inevitable, scruffy blue jeans, black leather jacket, and old snakeskin boots. The dude's another icon. His boots could have metal taps on the toes and heels, what do you think? That's it: a close-up of Álvaro's boots, walking away from Alicia; you hear the noise of the taps as the heels hit the asphalt... how do you like that? Heel and toe, heel and toe, a heavy effect, dense, like the steamy horizon. This is beautiful: metallic vipers slithering along under the desert sun, and in the background a slide guitar: slow blues. Here's another interesting title: *Iron Snakes*. Really powerful. It combines the idea of the reptile with the speed and toughness of the turn of the century; it alludes to industrialized and cybernetic society, the iron found in nature. But let's talk about the nature of the reptile: swift, aggressive and creeping. A viper can't survive by instinct alone; it needs armor. I like it. The only problem is that it might sound like science fiction or some cyberpunk bullshit, like all that modern crap you see nowadays. Well, we can leave it on stand-by for now; I'll decide later. Alicia casts a nonchalant glance to see what her he-man will do now that they're without a vehicle. The cops are on their tail and the coupe had been their freedom, with a six-cylinder boosted engine and a *Mad Max* style, to boot; I'm crazy about that, a dark effect that boosts its power all at once, thirty or forty percent. Whipping along at ninety-five per hour, every time Álvaro pulls on that magical gear shift, the coupe jumps to one twenty-five or one thirty-five. At that speed, the cops will be left behind in a flash, standing like posts in the middle of the road, a miracle worked by his friend Firulo, a wild man who lives for guns. With that beast roaring down the highway, they never would have caught them, but here, now, in this desert and this heat... "

"It would've been a good idea to check the water at the last gas station," Alicia interrupted absently, gazing at the horizon. She lit a cigarette with an old gray Zippo that she pulled from her purse, leaning against the trunk of the car, from where she observed Álvaro.

"It would've. That Zippo is going to have a place in my road movie, I'm telling you right now," Álvaro warned her, sticking one finger in the field of the lens. He was filming the scene with his camera. And his camera was looking at Alicia; it looked at her as she took out the cigarette, as she flicked the Zippo. As the tip lit up, he zoomed in on an extreme close-up of her overly plump, red lips. When she turned her back, annoyed, he kept filming her and said with a relentless expression:

"Alicia avoids the subjective camera of Álvaro's fierce gaze. She smokes nervously, remembering the switchblade in the man's jeans, but above all, she thinks about the thirty-eight nesting in his jacket, the thirteen notches engraved on its mother-of-pearl handle. That weapon has been with him for as long as they've been together, maybe even longer. And it has a sweet, obedient trigger. On the other hand, the edge of the switchblade nauseates her; it's quite capable of cutting through a high-voltage cable. Yeah, Alicia doesn't screw around with Álvaro, who's now resting against the nose of the coupe. He's deep in thought, as silent as a cobra, or anyway, a scorpion. A scorpion's better. Ry Cooder is playing when Álvaro turns to gaze toward the south. Extreme close-up of his intense black eyes, fixed on the road. Those eyes reflect what they see: nothing. He turns his head gently and seems to concentrate. Alicia is well acquainted with his keen hearing. Yes, something's coming; it's like a buzzing sound, moving along, something vague that can't yet be differentiated from the sounds of insects, the dehydrated breeze. It can only be a decent-sized engine that's still out of sight. It's not a car, not a truck, either, because the cargo bed would have already appeared like a small, square bulk slicing the horizon. Enormous trucks, trailers, cross that desert, transporting... something, I don't know, alfalfa or bootleg whiskey, it doesn't matter much right now. And it's not that Álvaro knows the area—as he explained to her with a raised index finger that sketched something in the air and then suddenly pointed at the woman's chest—it's simple perception. There aren't any fields there for trucks to pass by with sheep, and no family four-by-fours looking for a place to camp and hang out their snot-nosed shitty kids' dirty diapers. The wind comes from the south, carrying the sound of the machine that's already outlined on the horizon; you can see it, its silhouette is like a burnt, smoking match that comes along down the highway, disappears from view into a hollow and reappears a moment later. A black match with silvery sparks that comes thundering through the air a mile away and approaches at the same speed can be only one thing: a Harley is coming; no other machine can make its presence known like that."

"You're wrong," said Alicia, who had already stubbed out her cigarette. The filter tip peeked out halfway from the sand. "We don't need your road movie. Just a phone or the decision to walk. We'll find something. I'm not about to spend the rest of my life here while you present your film at the Sundance Festival, darling. Get down before the eagles nab you."

"I don't know if I should take that as a compliment, sweetheart. I fly high, and this desert inflames my muses. Stop kidding around—a nice truck with a gaucho inside will come along soon and give us a lift—you, me, and the coupe. It looks like the end of the world, but it's just a road where twenty percent of cars have some kind of breakdown. Statistics, my love, those things that bore you so much. It's true there are no gas stations, nobody has come by in the last fifteen minutes, also true, but people live here, even though you don't see them. And sooner or later they'll come along in their nice little trucks to distribute their country crap: fruit, pigs, and beans. End of story. And now, woman, you're about to surrender to male dominance," Álvaro announced, as he unbuttoned his jeans and walked over to her, assuming his famous monstrous-perverter-of-schoolgirls expression.

"Elizabetha, *I give you eternal life*," Álvaro recited, displaying his incisors. And he was Gary Oldman, no doubt about it.

"Come out of there, idiot." Alicia laughed. "They'll see us here." She was still laughing, with her virginal face. And, of course, she was Wynona Ryder.

"So much the better, because then they'll come over and rescue us, you rebel female. I have to teach you your lesson for the day," Álvaro said, drooling, making obscene noises, and licking his lips. "And if someone's watching us, my exquisite Transylvanian bride, let them enjoy it: let's give 'em a good show. I've crossed oceans of time to find you, never forget that, Elizabetha, oh, my beloved, you remind me of glorious battles against the Turkish invaders; my sword rises in your honor."

High-angle view that zeroes in on Alicia's feline features, detects the tip of her tongue peeking out between her bloated, flame-colored lips, her gesture of submission and desire before the majestic emergence of her man. She half-closes her eyes and falls backward into the coupe's rear seat. Álvaro crawls between her legs, now bare, his pants halfway down. Giggles burst out in the clear, dry air. Fifteen minutes later, an intemperate *ahem* interrupts their demonstration of affection.

"Ahem." It sounded like an explosion followed by a brief throat clearing.

The lovers were startled. Álvaro leapt up; his erection, which wouldn't last more than another few seconds, was still viable. He pulled up his jeans—clumsily—while he studied the intruder's gaze at Alicia's nakedness. She covered her hips as best she could with Álvaro's shirt; her pants, as red as her overflowing lips, rested in the middle of the asphalt.

"And where'd *you* come from?" Álvaro asked in a smothered voice, noting the man's bicycle beneath his crotch.

"Sorry to interrupt, caballero. It's just that I thought you needed help, and... oh, excuse me, I meant with the car, no offense."

At that point, through maneuvers of excessive modesty,

Álvaro's shirt produced a strange torsion on Alicia's hip, and a dark patch shone between her legs, as the gentleman now stared intently at the sky without letting go of his bicycle and sneaking furtive glances at the inside of the car.

Alicia adjusted her shirt as well as she could and got up onto her knees on the seat, her hands resting on Álvaro's shoulders, as she listened to the conversation with her best expression of composure.

"Have you been here a long time?" she asked, trying to avoid a new malfunction of her precarious wardrobe.

"I just got here. I was on my way home, and I saw the car with the hood raised, so then I thought you might have a problem, and I came over to see. Do you want me to call somebody?"

"Do you know a mechanic?"

"Not a real mechanic, no, but El Tolo can solve any problem. He fixes engines on boats."

"On boats," Álvaro confirmed, or asked.

"He's a mechanic and a sailor; his title is Naval Mechanic, that's how El Tolo makes his living. If you're in the middle of the ocean and your charter breaks down, you ain't gonna call the Auto Club, right?" The man laughed.

"And does El Tolo live far from here?"

"You gotta find him, but don't worry, I'm on my way to the pharmacist's house right now; he's got a phone, and we'll find him. He'll leave a message for El Tolo, and if nothing's come up at the last minute, he'll see you tomorrow without fail. How long will it take him to come? By this time of day tomorrow, give or take, you'll find him stretched out under your coupe. If El Tolo can't fix something, it can't be fixed, believe me, amigo. Nice car. You don't see beauties like that anymore."

"Not till tomorrow," Álvaro moaned. "What'll we do?"

"And where will we sleep?" Alicia asked.

"At the hotel," the man replied.

"What hotel?" asked Álvaro, convinced that the world was

empty for miles around.

"The Seagull, it's about two miles from here; just go straight, there's no way to get it wrong. Just a matter of starting to walk," he explained buoyantly.

"The Seagull, sailors... Two miles?"

"You got it."

"Along the main road?"

"Yes, señor."

"In the desert."

"We're *in* the desert, my friend. But make no mistake, there are sailors everywhere. Just the same, so you won't get lost, I'll tell you that the hotel is at the very end of town. It has red lights at the front door, you get what I mean; it's a by-the-hour hotel, excuse me, señora. All the kids go there. There's no way to get lost; even the village idiot knows where it is."

"Village? I didn't know there was a village around here. What's the town called, Don...?"

"Tanco, a pleasure. It's called Los Huemules, can you imagine? The town, I mean. Los Huemules—what a name, right? They say there were lots of 'em, seems like there was a whole herd of 'em, and they all ran around here. But I never saw one, never even seen the bones of a dead huemul, so I don't talk about that. They might've gone south, who knows, all those stories about migrations. Las Casas—that's what we call the town, you know, it's less formal, like it was before, when our parents founded it, and the truth is that it hasn't grown much, señor..."

"Álvaro is my name, and she's..."

"Alicia, I see," interrupted the man called Tanco.

"How'd you know?"

"Isn't that what it says on her T-shirt?"

Alicia didn't lower her eyes, but she knew that the man had gotten a good look at her skimpy, sweaty T-shirt. Her breasts were clearly visible beneath her printed name. And while modesty assailed her cheeks, she remembered almost incidentally that she was still squeezing Álvaro's shoulders, and that he hadn't abandoned his position between her and the man on the bike. The old guy's got quick eyes, her thoughts resounded through her brain like a horn. Not to mention, he had enjoyed a free show for who knows how long, fucking old fart, the horn concluded, leaving the matter closed.

"Tanco, Álvaro and Alicia: now we've been introduced. Thanks for your help, señor Tanco."

"That's how we are in Las Casas, señora." The man touched the edge of his beret and took off pedaling toward the ravine. Álvaro stood there watching him for a moment, listening to Alicia protest and get dressed at the same time. He was thinking about his Harley approaching from the same place, when Alicia snorted directly into his ear.

"Are you listening to me? Hand me my pants, please."

Álvaro looked at Alicia's red pants, lying on the road beneath the sun's rays.

"Who's gonna see you?" he said.

KYRIE

1) GARBAGE, SEAGULLS, AND RAT'S PAWS

They had walked about two miles; now they're walking another two, and then they're going to walk yet three more. They assumed that the town remained behind them, but since there were no obvious reasons to firmly believe that, they kept on going, chatting about movies and dirty old men and peeping Toms. Who could say if that Tanco guy calculated distances better than they did; the asphalt never ended and neither did their trek. They saw no indications whatsoever. They looked for a gas station, for example, always so likely to be close to towns, near by-the-hour hotels, or some sign that said Los Huemules 1½ miles or Welcome to Los Huemules, or at least a lousy arrow. There was no traffic light, either, or—best case scenario—a blinking neon sign to identify the Seagull Hotel, that scene from *Psycho*, Álvaro explained—marking the arrival at the Bates Motel. Of course their arrival should have taken place at night, but that was another story. And since there was nothing, they decided to keep going, assuming that an indie film director like Álvaro and a street theater actress like Alicia (she of the sweaty, ostentatious breasts, fuck that old creep Don Tanco, anyway), would have little sense of the road already traveled.

"Fucking old creep," Alicia said, flicking her tongue.

"What?" Álvaro asked, designing frames and tracking shots as Ry Cooder and his slide guitar played in the background. His gaze was a lens that took in Alicia's sandals, dragging painfully along the hot asphalt below and to his right. Stones were scattered along the road, troubling their steps. Álvaro and Alicia were wounded, fleeing from the police; it's an epic escape, smiled Álvaro, who, without metal taps or snakeskin boots, and seeing Alicia's pathetic sandals, thanked God for his Nike Airs.

"Why'd you say that?" he asked, aware of the comfort of his own feet and pierced with pity for the state of Alicia's sandals. Maybe he should have offered to... what? Carry her through the air? Sure, why not. Hoist her up on his shoulders? Maybe, for a while. What right did he have to be walking along so comfortably when his wife couldn't? Who did he think he was—Woody Allen? He would have given an arm to be Woody Allen. Pick her up horsey-style?

"You could pick me up horsey-style," Alicia literally spat as she walked by. Álvaro stopped in his tracks, watching her walk. From behind he could see the angle of her that he liked best, supported by two legs that he adored and the soles of her feet suffering the rigors of the desert like the Apostles. Alicia from behind was his downfall.

"What did you say?"

"Nothing, I'm reading your thoughts. And before I said 'fucking old creep.' But if you're interested, even before that, I said that must be the garbage dump over there."

"How can it be a garbage dump? What are you talking about? Garbage dumps never come before towns because they scare away the tourists. Don't talk nonsense."

"And where do you suppose so much garbage came from? Nobody cares about tourism here. Don't be so naïve. Besides, there were seagulls, you can believe me. I have better eyesight than you."

"Alicia, Alicia, there are no seagulls in the desert. They need water, darling. Just a little. And I don't know where the garbage comes from; maybe they cart it in on trucks. Who'd be stupid enough to unload garbage by their own door? Use your head, sweetie."

"Why would they call that shithole hotel that never appears the Seagull? Fuck that old man and all the huemules. Hey, can you explain *that* mystery of life to me?"

"It must be because I didn't check the water in the coupe."

"Don't come looking for me because you'll find me, Álvaro. I'm in a terrible mood."

"It's obvious, sweetheart. And let me remind you that the sun will go down soon."

"All the better. I must be bright red by now."

"Like your pants. And like your cherry-colored lips, woman. And while we're on the subject, let me tell you that when the sun goes down in the desert, even the huemules freeze their asses off."

"You could have told me sooner; I left my sweatshirt in the car."

"I just thought of it. Look—let's do this: I'll follow your hunch and we'll go back and look for your garbage dump. If you, Milady, can show me that what you saw were real, undeniable seagulls, then, love of my life, I promise to look like crazy for the hotel so you won't be cold and you can take a nice, hot shower and then watch some porn flick, cuddled up with your man, both of us drinking delicious, foot-pressed local wine, straight from *The Grapes of Wrath of the Desert of the Lost Huemules*. Do you like the program, my love?"

Alicia didn't reply, or maybe her reply was the expressionless nod that became noticeable every time she passed Álvaro now headed straight toward the garbage dump, where they would arrive nearly two hours later, she announcing how cold she was despite being wrapped in Álvaro's leather jacket, even with his socks and handkerchief around her neck, but not his

Nike Airs because they were too big for her and because the exchange would have left him barefoot, a situation that would have been clearly unthinkable, and one to which he remained happily resigned and grateful, though if she had asked for them, he would have capitulated as an extreme form of consolation, Álvaro thought, with just a few doubts about his munificence. Just as he had maintained before and reaffirmed at this very moment, Alicia noted two crucial matters behind the second garbage heap:

1) Seagulls were flying around, despite the impending darkness, some of them circling in the air, others picking through scraps, and,

2) Behind a curve sprinkled with what looked like seagull shit, white feathers and refuse from the town, twinkled some red lights, incomprehensibly far from the main road, to greet the weary traveler;

"*Quod erat demonstrandum*, my queen, I bow before your wisdom and admit I have no defense, and therefore I turn over my king, checkmate, stop, I throw in the towel, raise my white flag, lay down my arms: This is my unconditional surrender. What can I do to keep your rage from being unleashed on my poor, addled head? But let's make it clear: even though this seagull business may explain the name of the hotel, it's still a logical flaw," admitted Álvaro, infuriated, but still listening to Ry Cooder, this time as the musical background to what felt like reaching refuge at last.

They entered the hotel. It was growing dark. From the reception area you could see an avenue tinted yellow by the iodine lamps, some lit, others flickering, that stood out against the tops of the ancient trees. Even though it was still early—maybe 7 PM—there was little traffic. A small truck coming from a side street crossed the road two blocks farther down, where the avenue dipped, only to climb one block later. There was the hint of a square on the right, suggesting that the city limits began there: the church, perhaps a movie theater and a bar. Farther down, the lights were missing or had gone out after blinking for God knows how long. Beyond the square, the avenue was a large shadow. A wall calendar, if no one had forgotten to pull of the pages, would have revealed that it was Monday, which seemed a reasonable enough explanation for such a lack of action.

"Today's Monday." Once again Alicia read his mind. "But there ought to be someone to take care of people in this flea-bag."

"If they have the nerve to cross the garbage dump. Who's gonna come here to spend the night? Please explain that mystery to me," said Álvaro, clapping his hands in the local style and trying to squeeze his head through the little window.

"A hot-sheet hotel has to be discreet. I get that this is asking a lot around here, but it's gotta be pretty tough to hole up in an inn without everyone, including the greengrocer, finding out."

"Standard or deluxe?" The voice came from behind the window without revealing a face, which must have been an attempt at discretion, quite understandable and sensitive to Alicia's reasoning.

"Deluxe," she said at the same time Alvaro answered "Standard"—an obvious mistake that he rectified instantly: "Deluxe." And then, turning to her:

"You deserve it." And then, addressing the voice behind the window: "There's TV, I suppose?"

"There are erotic films on Channel Three. The costumes in the trunk are free. It's fifty pesos a trick."

"Fifty pesos. And for the whole night?" Álvaro asked, at the brink of desperation.

"One hundred pesos. Are you going to take it, señor?"

"Yes," Alicia accepted, holding out her hand for the key. Then she looked at Álvaro, until he pulled out two bills and handed them over to the dim voice. They spied a little rat's paw that dropped the key and whisked away the bills in a single movement. Then the voice said:

"Second floor, room two-oh-two."

2) ALICIA BEHIND THE LOOKING GLASS

On entering the room, nothing felt unusual, except for the notion of a temporary shelter in the desert, behind a garbage dump inhabited by seagulls at the entrance to a town that seemed too empty at seven in the evening. The décor was predictable: many mirrors with many scratches, red and blue lights; the TV and music controls were to the right of the bed, which was covered with an old charmeuse bedspread. A chair that resembled a small divan, slightly reclined, suggested an erotic game not entirely devoid of ingenuity. To one side was the costume chest: later, together, they would open the lid, made of remarkable painted cardboard. She noticed, because she always noticed, that the curtains were heavy, they looked like dusty brown corduroy, and they were drawn. Behind them, a window with closed blinds and an air conditioner that didn't work completed all the elements of interest. You couldn't exactly say the atmosphere was oppressive; there could have been some form of ventilation that wasn't in plain sight, though, in any case, the smell of room deodorizer was strong. They devoted some time to discussing whether the scent was tobacco cover-up or something floral and finally agreed: it smelled like a fleabag motel.

Álvaro went around inspecting the corners, searching for electrical outlets behind the TV to connect his camera. And he recorded, too, rather randomly: he turned the machine on and off again. When Alicia went into the bathroom and flicked on the light, a mirror turned transparent, and she got ready to shower while Álvaro carefully devoted himself to recording the scene. He was careful to keep silent: she didn't like it when he spied on her, and if she had known, she would have screamed bloody murder about the violation of her modesty and other female qualities. She would sooner have invited him to join her in the shower or turn his face—the camera's lens, in this case—toward her and film right in front of her, as she wasn't about to deprive him of a nice dance—the kind where you can leave your hat on. Because it wasn't a question of nudity, but rather of staring. Now Álvaro thought that when his turn came, he'd have to make sure the mirror didn't become transparent again so that Alicia wouldn't discover the truth on tape. There'd have to be a button to fix that, he thought, as he kept on recording happily. He used the zoom feature, took note of details; overcome with excitement he changed angles, aerial view and worm's-eye view, tracking movements. Head and shoulder shots: the camera traced her hand moving to the T-shirt she wore with ALICIA inscribed in front, her delicate fingers opening in a quick pincer movement to let the t-shirt fall; now one foot abandoned its sandal, then the other, followed by an exaggerated concentration on her pants, which slid with difficulty down the curve of her hip, one leg emerging, then the other.

One scene: Alicia from the rear, looking at herself in the mirror, while the shower warms the room and a light bulb on the medicine cabinet outlines her silhouette, backlighting her as she brushes her black, luxuriant hair, the endless curls.

He took note of the woman's distant air, holding on to the power of having captured what she would never know, while the sharp pleasure of Olympic heroes spurred his pupils on, adding eagerness to the voyeur's gaze. Now Alicia, the ingénue, stepped into the shower and soaped herself while Álvaro, the villain—like Actaeon spying on Diana, impassioned by the risk of being seen at the very moment of seeing, that mad defiance of the gods—recorded without a pause: the soap and water slipping down her trembling breasts, her bony shoulders, nibbled so many times, then a turn, and now it was her back, culminating in the ever-privileged realm of dreams. Alicia's fleeting gesture would end the moment her hand appeared between her legs: her pubic hair dripped endlessly and the woman's head bent slightly downward as the sponge stopped for a little longer than anticipated: it had been a private, exclusionary pause, accompanied by the humming of a tune that vaguely resembled something they had heard on a local radio station when they were still in the car, traveling.

Alicia turned off the faucet and stretched her hand out to the towel rack, and still humming, began to dry herself. Álvaro turned the camera off.

SEQUENTIA

{III}
DIES IRAE

AT DAWN, REASONABLY enough, a rooster crowed. The hotel room had been booked till noon, but the rooster was almost a mystical experience, and Álvaro opened his eyes. What he saw sweetened his waking moments: the costumes, rustic but well-employed until daybreak, were now scattered on the floor. The gown of a poor but honorable princess slept entwined with a pair of fitted, red workout pants, with devil mask included. Beyond that was the camera, which had stopped recording at some point, while they slept, exhausted, sweet-skinned, loosely embraced. The bed reeked of sex. He smiled.

Alicia wasn't there.

Álvaro checked the time and assumed she was in the bathroom. As he was drifting off to sleep again, he managed to notice that the mirror had not turned transparent. At a quarter to ten the buzzer went off. He picked up the phone receiver, and Little Rat's Paw announced that breakfast was about to end. He thanked him, said he'd be right down, and hung up.

"Rise and shine, my peasant princess," he called to his wife, asleep behind him. He turned to his right.

Alicia wasn't there.

The bathroom mirror was still opaque. He got up and looked around the room, disoriented, thinking that there weren't many possibilities of finding anything unusual, since everything was in plain sight. Alicia's clothes were missing. Therefore, she must have gone out at some point after the rooster crowed, while he was in the bathroom with the un-transparent mirror. He went to the bathroom, flipped the light switch, and the mirror went transparent again. He didn't understand: he supposed she must have gone downstairs for breakfast. He picked up the receiver and asked for his wife. Little Rat's Paw informed him that he hadn't seen her, though discretion always proved that it was better not to look too closely, but breakfast was served in a bar around 200 yards from the hotel; maybe the lady was there. Way-station motels never have a dining room on the premises, señor, the man explained. Álvaro hung up, went into the bathroom and showered, feeling that no one was watching him from the other side of the mirror. He dressed quickly and went downstairs to breakfast. Alicia must have been having a coffee with bread and butter and reading the news in the local paper, bored and eager to head home and be done with this creepy trip. He agreed with her and decided that would be the first thing he would tell her when he saw her: Let's hope that guy El Tolo knows how to fix the car and we'll go home. I'm tired of the desert and of hidden rat's paws. He walked the 200 yards to the little bar. Alicia wasn't there.

He felt strange. What am I doing in this place; what do I have to do with these people? I want to go home. He sat down at a table and the waiter came.

"Buenas," the waiter greeted him. "Are you coming from the Seagull?"

"Buen día. Yes, here's the key. By any chance have you seen a woman with black, curly hair and red pants? She's wearing sandals and a T-shirt that says ALICIA," Álvaro asked.

The waiter made a face and seemed to think for a long time while Álvaro wondered how many strange women with black curls and red pants could have passed through that place, at that hour, in that crappy town. Only one, he concluded, when the waiter said:

"Yeah, she was here about an hour ago." Álvaro listened, feeling that at least he was starting to get his bearings.

"An hour. And did you see which way she went?"

"She went with El Tolo, I think, to get her Chevy fixed, probably. Calm down, maestro, I don't think there's anything seriously wrong. That car's tougher than nails."

Álvaro did what the waiter advised: he calmed down, believing there was nothing wrong with the car, that his iron coupe was indestructible and that his wife... what reason could she have had for going out on the main road with a stranger, even if it was to get the car fixed? She always ended up in trouble, and then he had to go rescue her. Alicia didn't know the meaning of the word fear; she was capable of getting involved in any situation by trusting her instinct, because people are good and if there were some dangerous bad guys around, it was clearly a social problem having to do with the oppressed, those excluded by the system, so it was a matter of starting a revolution, or making some sort of change like that. Before anything was said, she would recommend the firing squad for the majority of those who oppressed the people. It didn't make much sense to her politically, but she didn't make great distinctions.

The café con leche arrived with some toast that turned out to be regrettable. Álvaro finished his breakfast, smoked a cigarette, and decided to go back to the hotel. He still had three hours left on their room reservation, but he didn't have too much confidence in those people. So he checked the room to make sure he hadn't forgotten anything, looked under the bed, in the bathroom and in the closet, picked up his things, and when he was about to leave he noticed Alicia's little bag, still slung over the back of a chair. She hadn't even taken that with her. He checked the time, then glanced out at the avenue and realized that an unbearable wait lay before him. Then, as he noticed that the window of the room was open, when last night it had been closed and with the blinds lowered, and at the same time he minimized the importance of that detail, he decided to cross the garbage dump to look for his wife. And for his car.

He walked along the road, toting his camera and Alicia's bag. He was wearing his leather jacket. It wasn't too hot yet; he tolerated it well. It was better than carrying it in his hand. He looked straight ahead, hoping she would appear any minute, though he still had nearly two more miles to go. He imagined his wife—with a *stranger*—in her sexy T-shirt, already remarked upon by Don Tanco, there, in the middle of the desert, raped or—even worse—seduced. He couldn't help it: that woman drove him out of his mind with her naïveté. Who was that Tolo guy to decide to accompany her alone? And why the hell hadn't she awakened him? Fixing car's was a man's job. What did she understand about radiators and broken piston rods? Didn't she know how fucked up people can be? She didn't know. She'd always been that way And there was no reason to think anything was going to change now.

He walked along, and the sun rose noticeably in the light and on his back. He was sweating but still determined to put up with the jacket. The asphalt was an infinite tape; it stretched to the end of the universe and then folded downward. When he climbed a hillside, he managed to see the rounded horizon. Some rat-sized arachnids crossed the road before him, black and swift. He stopped, watched them disappear into the sand, and the sweat on his back grew cold, turning into gooseflesh. He never could stand spiders, if indeed that's what those horrid beasts were. A phobia, that's what it was called, a stupid, irrational fear in the presence of any type of small, black thing that walked on more than four legs. All bugs were dangerous, no matter what the reason, but especially these, because the car was broken and they belonged to another ecosystem. Now two more came along, one of them bigger. He took a step backward and thought that there might be more of those creatures behind him, but he didn't dare look. Aliens, that's what they were, scary monsters who inhabited the desert space, scurrying from right to left, that ran away, not so much out of fright, but rather determined to camouflage themselves among the terrifying blackberry bushes, ready to stalk and ambush him. Maybe they were already settled in his car, and when he tried to leave—*with Alicia*, because when he had her within reach of his hands and his fury, he was going to pick her up, scream his head off and then, without asking her anything and violating all her progressive feminist rights, he was going to toss her into the car like a doll and speed home, never letting the speedometer dip below 110 mph—those repulsive desert aliens would start to attack them, crawling like ghostly emanations out of the air conditioning vents, the nozzles, from between the seat cushions.

He kept on walking, watching the little black monsters cross one way and another, and feeling increasingly angry at his wife. After a while he saw a blinding light. He approached, and the flash took on a red color and then a shape: his coupe. It was still on the edge of the road, tilted toward the left side. He tried to detect movement, but the coupe seemed just as lonely as he had left it the day before. He quickened his pace, planted the camera on his shoulder and turned it on. The zoom revealed the same amplified image. Alicia wasn't there. He walked even faster, and when he was close by, El Tolo slid out from under the car: a beefy man who stood up and then leaned over the engine. Then he straightened up and saw Álvaro approaching, waved to him, climbed into the car and started the engine, which responded with a painful groan. He tried again, and once more: a metallic, toneless squeak. The man called El Tolo got out of the car, waved at him again, shrugged and gestured. Álvaro understood that whatever was wrong with his car was complicated. He continued to look around, but Alicia wasn't there. She couldn't be behind the car, and there was nowhere else outside his visual field.

"Bad news!" El Tolo shouted. Álvaro rushed over.

"What are you telling me?" he asked, thinking of Alicia.

"A piston rod broke, caballero. It's going to need a complete overhaul. It'll take a few days."

Álvaro was less than ten yards away and was listening to

explanations about hard-to-find parts, old models, distances, delays in shipment arrivals, temporary fixes, an oil change.

"I understand my wife came here with you," Álvaro said or asked, and he was slightly stunned by the reply.

The man said that it wasn't true; he hadn't seen her, and he had the impression she'd chosen to return to the hotel to wait for Álvaro there. She had been in the bar. El Tolo had heard from unnamed sources, and according to those same sources, at first she had mentioned her intention of going with the mechanic in the hope of driving the car back to the hotel and surprising her husband with a fix as quick as it was impossible, given its recent inspection, but later it became clear that she had given it more thought and had gone back to wake him. To wake *him*, Álvaro? That's what they told El Tolo, at least. No, not the waiter at the bar, local people. What people, who? Álvaro insisted. You don't know them, what's a name mean to you? What matters is what I said I heard: she went back to the hotel to wake you.

"To wake me, but how, if I went to the hotel bar and I never saw her at any time?"

Maybe she had gone out shopping then, El Tolo postulated. In Las Casas there was a place that sold local products that might have been interesting for any young woman: crafts, candies, trinkets. He could relax: nobody got lost in Las Casas, he said.

"You can relax, don—nobody gets lost in Las Casas." El Tolo was speaking, and now he pointed out his motorcycle, resting behind the car, with a gesture that indicated he needed to return to town for the pickup to carry the coupe to the repair shop. Álvaro could stay at the hotel, but El Tolo recommended a trustworthy pensión, twenty pesos a night, including breakfast and lunch, but dinner was cheap. There was nothing else to wait for. And now that I think of it, said El Tolo, smacking himself on the forehead, yeah, what a jerk I am, how could I not have mentioned it, you know, thing is, when I'm under a car I forget about everything, excuse me, don, they told me in passing, it was just when I was on my way here, and like you can see, I didn't remember it, I must be losing my memory, but anyway, they told your wife about the pensión. Who? Álvaro asked. Someone, jefe, don't worry, they explained to her that any part takes at least a day to get here, so now you know she wasn't so optimistic about the car, and so she asked if there was somewhere cheaper, in case you needed to stay longer, and they gave her that information, a good place, home style cooking, a good price, she must've gone directly there, for sure, maestro, that's why you didn't see her. It's down there, on the avenue, right on the square, El Tolo said, and Álvaro calmed down; Alicia was in the pensión, of course, it was all clear now; she had been worried about the price. Almost smiling, Álvaro thanked her for her consideration. The car could be repaired, he heard El Tolo say, for not too much money, nobody has money here, not like in the capital, so he could leave everything to El Tolo. He took the recommendation and put himself in El Tolo's hands, he accepted the man's instructions and hopped on the back of the motorcycle. The man gave a kick and the machine purred happily; they looped around and took off. The coupe was alone once more.

{IV}
TUBA MIRUM

BUT ALICIA WASN'T at the pensión. And the owner, El Tolo's wife, a fat woman named Fabiana in a greasy blouse and jeans as wide as a tent, said she had never seen her, though it must have been the same woman who, she'd been told, was sunbathing in the square. She was reading, propped up against an ancient oak tree, they'd said, and nobody knew her.

"She was reading. What could she have been reading if she doesn't have anything to read?" Álvaro stupidly asked, Alicia's little purse dangling from his shoulder with all her belongings inside.

"How should I know, señor? But do something—drop off her things in the room and go to the square. The town's not so big; she's likely closer than you think Nobody gets lost here. Where could she go? Walk a little and you'll be back in the desert. Listen to me, go to the room, freshen up a little, calm down, and go look for your wife. I'll bring you a coffee," Señora Fabiana suggested or ordered; there was no arguing with her, and Álvaro didn't have the strength to turn down the offer. He went to the room, left his camera on the double bed, went to the bathroom to freshen up and tried to calm his nerves. When he emerged, there was a tray with coffee on the night table. It was steaming. He sat down on the bed obediently and drank all the coffee. When he had finished, he realized that he'd forgotten to add sugar.

Still obedient, he went out looking for his wife. The square was one block away; he walked. And no sooner had he stepped on the dry grass, he saw the oak tree, but Alicia wasn't there. He spent a moment looking over the place. A few kids were playing in the sandbox; a horse grazed in the square; the town hall seemed empty. Two women with white kerchiefs on their heads entered the church. To one side there was a little bar with a few customers inside drinking wine and playing truco, or so it seemed to him. He crossed the street and headed for the bar. As he walked in, El Tolo came by in his pickup truck and honked happily at him.

The clientele looked at him. They were playing tute, or maybe truco. He didn't understand a thing about card games.

"Buenas," he greeted them and walked over to the counter. The bartender observed him with a sour expression.

"What can I get you?" said the man. Álvaro thought for a moment and ordered gin, just a small glass. He hated gin, especially at this time of day, but he needed to curry favor.

"They tell me my wife was around here; it seems she was seen reading under the oak tree. A curly brunette. Do you know anything about it, jefe?" The bartender handed him the glass, from which he took a small, quick swig. He tried to conceal his grimace and felt ridiculous drinking an alcoholic beverage that he liked even less than the guy behind the bar.

"Go ask at the police station; nobody's been in here," was the delayed, dry, and offhand reply.

Álvaro heard "police station" and realized that this business was getting worse. The guy's expression was a combination of I don't know a thing and I don't give a shit. He turned toward the customers.

"Anyone seen anything?"

They looked at him, cards in their hands, garbanzos on

the table, the small wine glasses refilled. One man smoked a cigar, hand-rolled in a corn husk; another, a dark tobacco cigarette, unfiltered. All of them wore canvas shoes, some of them frayed, no-name jeans, and high-waist farmer's pants, raggedy T-shirts, yellowish, nicotine-stained mustaches. And all of them were missing teeth.

One of them, who had a luxuriant beard and was downing something transparent, wore a tilted black beret. Álvaro thought of Che Guevara and was angered by the liberties his mind took.

"Why don't you have a seat and tell us about it," the man in the beret invited.

"If your missus isn't here, she's gotta be somewhere. In Las Casas…"

"No one gets lost, I've already heard that," Álvaro finished the sentence, ill-humoredly.

"Okay, don't get upset. I understand your position, but the fact is, nothing could've happened to her. We're in Los Huemules, caballero; this is a town of work and peace, understand? We're all good folks here; of course we'll help you. Manolo, another drink for the gentleman, on me. You need to calm down."

Álvaro was about to refuse the drink, but he didn't want to step on anyone's toes. When Alicia showed up, he'd send them all to hell and the two of them would go home without even stopping for a cup of coffee. He drank the second gin and told them what they already knew: the broken-down car, the night at the hotel, the vanished woman. By the end of the story, dizzy from the gin and the heat, he remembered he was walking around on an empty stomach. He asked what time it was. Two, they told him, and he thought how things weren't going right for him. He had gotten up at 9:30, a quarter of ten at the latest, and he hadn't found his wife. Where could she have gone in all that time? He longed to see her, embrace her, cover her face with kisses. He swore that he'd never get angry at her again. All he hoped for was for her to tell him where she'd gone. Not even that—it would be enough for her just to show up. All he wanted was to go back home. He asked for something to eat, anything. They brought him a salami and cheese sandwich. He ate it guiltily, grieving for Alicia, had more gin, and plunged into his thoughts, as he listened to a distant noise that sounded like the chattering of a parrot. "Go see the mayor," the parrot seemed to say, and Álvaro thought of Alicia, if she were to return, he thought, his attention drifting, the weight of the universe would once again be shared between them. "He didn't hear me," he heard someone say.

"I didn't hear you say what?" He reacted with a start, dizzy, and with the taste of pig fat on his lips. The crusty bread dropped thousands of crumbs on his jeans, his jacket, his Nike Air sneakers.

"I'm telling you to go see the mayor. He oughta know what to do when these strange things happen. And if not, then go to the pensión to rest and leave it all to me. Anyway, the mayor naps in the afternoon, so you go and get some sleep too, and so will I. At five I'll run over to the house and when you wake up, we'll have something more solid, okay?"

"What's the mayor going to do?" Álvaro held out his pack of blond tobacco cigarettes, but no one accepted. He took out Alicia's Zippo and lit up. A knot formed in his throat, and he ran his left hand through his hair.

"Well, maybe he'll know something more. I don't know what to tell you, maestro; nothing ever happens here."

Álvaro hesitated for a moment, realized he was falling apart; he wasn't getting anywhere like this. He needed to calm down. And he thanked them for the gesture, shook the hand of the man in the beret, tried to pay, but they wouldn't let him, said goodbye to all of them and went back to the pensión. As he crossed the square, he saw the two women in white kerchiefs coming out of the church.

{V}

REX TREMENDAE

THE MAN IN THE beret, Romano—that's how he introduced himself, with just his last name—was one of the mayor's henchmen, a guy who went around every day testing the social atmosphere, to find out if there were any arguments, complaints, things like that: a political operator, he explained. Because the mayor liked to stay in contact with his town, and Romano was in charge of making that work. He had told the mayor about Álvaro's problem, and the mayor wanted to see him right away; the situation warranted it. Romano took him there in a Jeep and promised to pick him up later.

Álvaro, standing before a large, metal door, stopped and looked around.

The mayor's house was really the shell of an estancia that aspired to being a modest palace, something smaller than those Louis XV-style palaces, for example—a style it pompously imitated—with illusions of grandeur tarnished by a certain veneer of grease that didn't quite conceal the cracks left by shady money. It struck Álvaro as being too powerful, a strange kind of power. Los Huemules didn't seem like a wealthy place. A wrought iron fence surrounded what must have been four blocks around the hull of the estancia. Romano had informed him that the mayor's property continued behind the groves, that they formed a thick wall, reinforced with low, leafy shrubs, encircling the horizon. He must have spent a fortune on watering alone, given the dryness of the climate. The man restricted his movements to the house, and, in fact, never went out, not even to exercise his job responsibilities; he had moved the mayoralty to his bedroom, or something like that, Álvaro understood. In front of the house was a huge, rectangular Olympic swimming pool, some thirty meters long and with a double diving board at one end, a blue slide and stairs that plunged into the water at the other end, with several small tables all around, decorated with umbrellas. A boy jumped from the higher diving board, grabbing his knees cannonball style and hitting the water with a moderate splash, without being noticed by the two women who were sunbathing on chaises longues. He saw tennis courts, suspected the presence of an imposing barbecue area, adequate for large crowds, assumed the presence of imagined animals behind the leafy plants in back, in a space that resembled a forest, behind an artificial lake, complete with waterfall; it could have been a private zoo. In the middle of the park was the house—as they called it—with grand white stairs and an imposing door. The lavish windows were designed to resemble stained glass, and maybe they really were. Behind that, the guest house was barely visible; in the distance were the servants' quarters. There were dogs everywhere and personnel discreetly keeping watch.

He was greeted by a young woman in a maid's uniform, including cap. They entered. Álvaro thought of Xanadu as the maid guided him through endless corridors and majestic halls, until they reached an enormous room, decorated with paintings that must have been originals, but Álvaro didn't recognize any of them, and this fact made him strangely uneasy. He didn't understand what he was doing in this place. All he wanted was to take his wife back home.

The maid pointed to a half-open door on the other side of the room and let him proceed by himself. With each step his Nike Airs squeaked against the wood floor. There were quite a few huemul heads mounted on the walls. And hunting weapons: shotguns, rifles, pistols... The fact that there were pistols caught his attention; he'd never imagined they would be used to hunt animals. He walked through the door and there was the mayor, waiting for him.

The man must have weighed 400 pounds, he estimated, and he must have been around 6'6". He was lying on his right side; the hand holding up his cow-sized neck was like a column, and his belly, pushing into the space that separated them, was a heavy fallen sphere, a toppled cupola, resigned to its new function as a storage place for fat. The corpulent focus of the scene rested in a very expensive chaise longue, adorned with hardware in the form of eagles' heads in front and back, their necks descending and becoming feathery claws that rested on a carpet, almost certainly Persian. An Oriental-looking blanket and an unspecified number of thick pillows, decorated with golden tassels and squashed by the man's bulk, completed the adornments of that heavy chaise. In front of the mayor, a coffee table held heaps of empty, half-empty, and full dishes loaded with fast food, cold cuts, olives, bowls of little fried fish, peanuts, potatoes, assorted concoctions, pieces of chicken, bananas, melons, glasses half-filled with a golden beverage that might have been champagne, or white wine, or liqueurs, sodas, and bread, both in a breadbasket and outside of it, at various stages of consumption, whole, chewed, in bits, remains of triple-deckers and other kinds of sandwiches, pita and sliced bread, and a profusion of crumbs scattered here and there. Behind him, a 65-inch TV screen showed a soccer game, most likely European. Someone seated in a chair with its back to Álvaro channel-surfed between that and another sports channel that was showing an NBA basketball game, but all Álvaro could see of him was his right hand manipulating the remote. To one side of the mayor, a very short woman, perhaps a dwarf, assisted him, dried his interminable sweat, offered him drinks, and plied him with little snacks, one after another. During her brief breaks, she knitted something that looked like a robe or a tablecloth. Evening was falling and the heat didn't let up, despite the air conditioning—it seemed they had set it on low—and the ceiling fan that hung directly above the fat man.

When Álvaro introduced himself, he felt a temptation to bow. It was just for a moment, as if his impulse had frozen midway between standing and bending over. The fat man barely looked at him, but the tiny woman stopped her knitting at a particular stitch, held the yarn and needle in one little hand and the fabric in the other, but didn't raise her eyes. When he sat down, she resumed knitting.

A silence fell. The commentator's voice remarked on the goalie's anguished expression at the penalty shot they were about to take.

"Good afternoon," Álvaro begin. "I'm here because my wife has disappeared and they tell me that by talking with you I might..."

"I've heard something about it," the mayor interrupted. "Tell me, young man, what were you and your wife doing around here?"

"We were traveling south; we were going to visit the lakes; we had rented a cabin. I wanted to work on my film script, and I always look for a peaceful spot to do that. I'm a film director."

The TV announcer shouted "Goooooooal!"and they lowered the volume a little. Álvaro managed to hear the word "Fantastic!"

"A film director? I see, very interesting. So tell me, have you filmed something I might've heard of, young man?"

"I don't think you'd know it. I make indie films; my movies circulate in universities, film clubs, even the occasional pirated video going around, and the truth is, that sort of thing makes me feel kind of proud. I haven't made too many films—a few short and medium-length ones. Nothing important."

"And what sort of films do you make?" There was a commercial break and the volume grew louder again. This was followed by an ad for a fail-proof weight loss program, available by phone; the contact number flashed across the screen with a recommendation to consult a doctor with any questions. Álvaro felt uncomfortable.

"Mostly dramas, realistic subjects, poverty in the cities, marginality. Kind of experimental. This time I was planning to do a road movie."

"A what?"

"A road trip movie. It's a genre—you know, like *Paris, Texas*."

"I don't know what that is. I don't think there's a road that goes from Paris to Texas; at least I've never heard of one. It must be a different kind of movie, one of those fantasy things with flying saucers, I suppose. Tell me, do you have a record?"

In the distance, the sports commentator could be heard: the second half was about to begin.

"You mean, do I have a résumé?"

The man grew stiff, if his back could assume such a position behind that tidal wave of fat.

"A criminal record," he explained, following a sigh that sounded like a tuba.

"A police record? What difference does it make?"

"Just stick to answering my questions, young man. I need to know who I'm talking to; don't you agree? In any case, I'm going to find out, don't worry, but it's better if you tell me yourself. It's a matter of trust."

Álvaro thought for a moment, took a deep breath, and said:

"Yes, in the neighborhood where I grew up, it's impossible not to have one. It's a very mixed atmosphere, people who were born there and people who had to move for economic reasons, lack of jobs, things like that. It ends up erasing the differences, and in the end it's all the same thing. We all had a file, and mine should be floating around there. My record, I mean."

He tried to look relaxed, but a dark tremor gnawed at his gut.

"What, exactly, is in your record?" insisted the fat man, tense, but friendly.

Behind them the channel surfing continued, there was music, and then a roar. The finger on the remote control stopped moving: someone had made a three-pointer. Álvaro thought it might have been Michael Jordan and felt an urge to look. He loved that player's moves.

"Nothing serious, señor. We were so young... One time my friends and I stole a car, to go for a joy ride. We were going to return it, but they caught us before we could. In my neighborhood that was just stupid kid stuff."

There was another silence; the woman stopped knitting, and someone hit the mute button on the TV. The fat man scrutinized him. The only noise was the sound of the fan blades spinning around.

"Were you driving?" the mayor asked.

"No, I didn't have a license. And there was also a brief hold with no arrest. I was fourteen, and my father came to pick me up at the police station. It might not even be in my file because I was a minor, but you see, I'm telling you anyway. As a matter of trust."

All at once the sound came back on, the woman picked up her needlework again, and the fat man said:

"It's good that you're telling me. Youthful pranks, sure, we've all done them. Anything else you want to add?"

"No, it gave me a good scare, and I never got involved in stuff like that again. Do you think something can be done?"

"About your record?"

"No, I'm talking about my wife."

"We'll see... Something can always be done if things are within the boundaries of the law. Why were you traveling along that deserted road?"

"I didn't know there was another one. It's the one I found on the map."

"That road's not on any map. I never authorized that."

"It's not? Then I don't understand; we probably got lost."

"Are you sure?"

"No, how can I be sure? I thought I was going along a road that…"

"It doesn't matter," the mayor interrupted. "What happened then?"

"With what?"

"With your car; don't ask idiotic questions." The mayor raised his voice, and the announcer lowered his.

"I didn't understand you. I don't know… something about the temperature, it seems. I think I didn't add water to the radiator, and, well, the piston rod broke."

"What kind of car is it?"

"A Chevy coupe, Seventy-six model, a good car. It's red, and it's never caused me a single problem. Well, until now."

"Who are you, young man?" The fat man's voice bore a tone of exasperation.

"I don't know what to tell you. My name is Álvaro, my wife is Alicia, I never get into trouble, I like indie films. I believe in God, but I don't take Communion. What do you want from me? Are you going to help me?"

He was trembling and couldn't hide it. He tried to light a cigarette, but the fat man held the palm of his hand up, and Álvaro put the pack away. The act of removing the cigarette from between his lips and replacing it in the package made him feel humiliated.

"All right then: we have a young couple traveling to the southern lakes, on their way to a cabin; they're going there to write a film script, everything's so idyllic, an old, famous-make car that breaks down on an abandoned road that doesn't show up on any map; a young man with a doctored police record—or something of the sort—who's a film director and doesn't get in trouble. I like that, and even more the fact that you're not an atheist, though you really should take Communion, because it's harmless and necessary. Fine. More than anything, I approve of your sincerity. Even though the subject matter of your films strikes me as trite, let me just say, that business about the downtrodden, well really, if you come from those sectors of society, it's possible that sort of thing might interest you for personal reasons, but if you want my opinion, it's a topic that doesn't work anymore. People need something different, more flags to fly, more things to fight for. The downtrodden have always been with us, but that doesn't mean it's worthwhile to repeat the same story. I hope you won't get the idea to film here without my permission."

"No, it never crossed my mind."

Álvaro felt somewhat more relaxed—and also more stupid. The trust that seemed to suddenly emerge from the guy calmed him, but it also gave him gooseflesh. It was like trusting a crocodile.

"And what time did you arrive?" the mayor asked.

"It must've been around seven, I think. Truth is, I didn't notice. It was getting dark. Yes, it must've been around that time. We were very tired, so we went to the room."

"Where?"

"At the hotel, the Seagull, the one behind… opposite the garbage dump."

"But why did you go there? You're married, I suppose."

"Um, no, we live together. I guess we're what you'd call common-law spouses. She's separated, but the divorce still isn't final, you know?"

"I see," said the mayor with an expression of distaste. The tiny woman handed him a tall glass with a blue drink and a little straw. Then she made a gesture to him that struck Álvaro as intimate. The woman, who didn't wear a uniform, wasn't a servant. She must have been his wife. The man helped himself to peanuts from a bowl on the chaise longue.

"Want some?"

"Some what?"

"Peanuts, a soda…" The mayor made a gesture. He was chewing, and some small fragments shot out of his mouth, little explosions of chewed peanut. Then he sipped his blue beverage. The ice cubes clinked.

"Thanks, I'm good."

"So, my friend, it's now been several hours since your… fiancée's been gone, and you're quite worried."

"Imagine," Álvaro admitted, feeling vaguely misunderstood and remembering the unrecognized original paintings.

"So… is it possible that she's left you?"

"I don't get what you mean." Now he thought about the huemul heads.

"It's obvious. Maybe she got tired of this adventure, of your broken-down car, and let's say, of not getting a good night's sleep. She could easily have thought she should've taken the boat, understand? Tell me it's not logical: you're sleeping like a log, the girl gets up early, goes to get some breakfast because, really, what's she going to do at the time of the morning in that dump where you decided to spend the night? She's not about to watch TV. Maybe someone offered to drive her somewhere, a gentleman with a car in good condition, very likely. I don't think a modern woman like that, who lives with a man without benefit of clergy, would have too many scruples about hopping into a stranger's car. Or possibly she just took a bus and went back home. It happens every day. Did you consider that possibility?"

"I don't believe she'd do that. My wife is… she isn't… That doesn't go along with her ideology."

Álvaro pronounced the word "ideology" and some part of him tensed.

"Okay, okay, I'm simply trying to evaluate possibilities so that I can think a little. Excuse me, I think I need to use the bathroom. Can you help me, my dear?" asked the fat man, looking at the tiny woman.

He stretched his hand toward her. The woman left off preparing a beverage and moved toward him. She offered him her scrawny hand—which reminded Álvaro of the little rat's paw at the hotel—and took the mayor's bestial one. Then she climbed up onto his legs and leaned backwards. They started to struggle: she pulled him toward her, and he tried to stand, but success took its sweet time. Then she struggled more. Álvaro noticed that her veins swelled up, and there was the sound of teeth gnashing. The mayor panted, gestured as if refusing; it looked as if he was about to raise himself, but he fell back down onto the chaise longue again, making a noise like a sack of potatoes. A new start: the tiny hand, tugging, panting, gnashing of teeth, gesture of refusal, sack of potatoes. The struggle lasted for a while, but Álvaro hesitated to offer his help, realizing that he was witnessing a more or less intimate scene. At last the man gave up.

"We'll leave it for later." He made another hand gesture, snorted, and returned to his clinking blue liquid.

"Tell me, what does your mistress look like? Jot this down, my dear."

The little rat pulled out a pad from somewhere, along with a diminutive, made-to-measure pencil, and prepared to take notes.

"She's five-four, more or less, light complexion, thick, black, curly hair, she's wearing red pants, a white T-shirt—it must be pretty dirty by now, the T-shirt, I mean—and it says ALICIA on her... um, on her chest, because that's her name, like I told you. She has on leather sandals and dark glasses, Marilyn-style."

"What?"

"The style, like the kind Marilyn Monroe, the actress, used to wear; they're like a face mask, you know? Black, with silver decorations at the ends. Very pretty retro sunglasses, I mean, old-fashioned, you understand. She's very pretty too; plus, she's an actress."

"How could I not know who Marilyn Monroe was? How old do you think I am?"

"I don't know how to guess people's ages, señor. I never could."

"So your girlfriend's an actress. How interesting. That could be very helpful. Is her face recognizable? Has she acted in any famous film?"

"No, she's only worked in mine. She was the lead."

"Ah, what a pity, but it's not so important. If she hasn't left Los Huemules, it won't be hard to find her, even if she fainted somewhere out there... but haven't you gone to the hospital yet?"

"I didn't think of it," Álvaro stammered.

"Look, I'm going to give you a piece of advice: Before you ask busy people for help, start with the simplest thing. If she were in the hospital now, that would solve everything. Does she have any kind of sickness?"

"No."

From far away in the living room came the sound of people shouting, cheering a team on. The tiny woman knitted and ripped out her stitches.

"Well, it doesn't matter; maybe she went for a walk and felt faint. That's a possibility. And if not, you'll need to go to the police station. You haven't done that either, I suppose."

"No, I came here because Romano, the guy in the beret, told me..."

"Don't do everything you're told; don't be naïve. When young people do what strangers tell them to do, they get into trouble, you understand that? I'm going to tell you something else: these aren't the best of times, for us, you know? Right here in Los Huemules, there's all kinds of stuff: people say things out of pure evil, people make up stories, they lie, just about everyone lies. You need a very firm hand to govern this fucking town, because if you don't, right away they form bands and they do stupid shit. Too much gin, ignorant people, they spend the whole day talking, they don't want to work, they earn a few pesos and off they go to the bar to play truco. You've seen them. Romano doesn't miss a thing, but it's better if you don't make me talk about that. Just look at how they drive people crazy with that business of the huemules. Did they tell you the story?"

"Tanco mentioned something, but I don't really remember, that they went south, I think it was, or that's what he thought, and he said he never saw the bones of a huemul. I don't know, maybe they're extinct. They're like deer, right? The truth is, it doesn't interest me. The only thing I want is to find my wife and go back home," Álvaro explained dispiritedly, feeling dazed.

The channel surfing went on furiously: incomprehensible sports, music cut off before it began, commercials, news briefs, the occasional movie in English, another one badly dubbed, and back to sports again.

"You see what I'm saying? Tanco barely knows you, and he's already talking crap. Imagine what they'll say after they've spent the whole night getting shitfaced. But I know how to rein them in. Look, young man, strange things are happening; it's not a good idea for you to go out at night. I know you'll think it's ridiculous, but life in the country isn't like in the city; people have different beliefs here. What're you gonna do, that's how they are. They talk so much crap, they believe in so many superstitions, they see a shadow and say it's the devil. And it's not without consequences, either you know: a guy who thinks he saw the devil, the next minute he's sure the devil's helper walks among the living—and then, watch out! If it was up to me, I'd have two or three of them shot, and send the others to do forced labor to make them learn. You can't make a silk purse from a sow's ear, and all that. They've ruined this country from the get-go, you know what I mean? Those people are like cows: the only thing they're interested in doing is chewing the same fucking cud all day long. But I'm changing that: I know it'll take a long time, but I'm prepared to give my life if necessary because I, señor, am a patriot, and my roots are healthy. A patriot is someone who's prepared to die at any time, because this country, my sincere and most excellent friend, was watered with the blood of men like me, in the first place, but also by cowards and traitors. There can never be too much blood spilled when the destiny of a nation is at stake, and it doesn't matter that we're talking about a little, two-bit town. The greatest fires start with a carelessly stubbed-out cigarette and end up destroying a whole province. When the fatherland calls, you've got to show up with your boots on, because God vomits out the half-hearted: never forget that. I'm going to give my life, just as my ancestors did, don't you doubt that for a minute, but before that happens, I'm going to clean up a few bad elements. I've got them all on my list; they're a bunch of dumb-ass half-breeds and drunks. Oh, God, I'll never understand these mixed couples—how can they stoop so low? More or less healthy people, immigrants, some from good lineage—I know all the families who built this town. And you watch them degenerate; they go to bed with anybody—Indian women, syphilitics, mulattoes with genetic defects, Gypsies, the mentally retarded, they even mate with Jewesses: as long as they have a hole between their legs, they're good enough, excuse my crudeness. They're like animals. They are animals. Mixtures like that corrupt the blood, and then they whelp these pieces of garbage that you've seen around here, sick people, Mongoloids, the feeble-minded—they're perverted monsters that go around drooling on themselves, caring only about the most disgusting activities, there in the square, masturbating right out in the open, monstrosities, all of them, God's vomit, which some good Christian has to clean up. And that's just one part of it. I could tell you about it all day long. That's what Romano does for me: he informs me of each and every detail, even though he bounces back and forth between the booze and his humanistic musings. But don't worry, he's on my list, too; if there's anything I can't stand it's those who hesitate. Bring me another drink, my love." The woman changed his glass and a fresh clinking of ice cubes could be heard.

"I like you: you're young and modern, and from what I

can see, you strike me as a healthy, well-educated, and sincere guy—especially sincere, that's good. You don't believe in what you don't see, although you do believe in God, which is a sign of a keen, lively intelligence. I'm not mistaken, am I? Heed my advice, young man, don't sink to the level of the rabble; don't listen to them and, above all, don't go out at night. Do me a favor—it's dangerous. And let's pray that your lovely young lady shows up before nightfall; I know what I'm talking about. You won't find anyone who knows more than I do about what goes on in town; that's why I'm the mayor. You'll hear from me soon. Go see the Chief of Police and tell him I sent you; go to the hospital, too. And a visit to the church wouldn't be a bad idea, either. I'm sorry you have to go. My dear, walk the gentleman to the door."

{VI}
RECORDARE

1) CRUELTY BEGINS AT HOME

Romano was waiting for him in the Jeep, looking at the entrance. He seemed anxious, smoking and drinking from a flask. He followed Álvaro with his eyes from the time he peeked out through the front door, as he approached along the gravel road, when they opened the gates for him, and till he sat down in the car. Then he directed his gaze ahead of him, turned on the engine and pulled away. They followed the road back in the midst of a self-conscious silence. At last the point man spoke:

"How'd it go?"

Álvaro hesitated before answering.

"I don't know if he's gonna help me. He seems like a guy who's"... Álvaro tried to avoid the word, but he gave in at last: "cruel. What do you think?"

"It's not a great idea to say that, señor. And I have no reason to listen to it. It's best not to give the mayor a bad impression of yourself. How did he like you, if I might ask?"

"He said he liked me, but I couldn't really say for sure."

"Believe him, he never lies. What possible reason could he have to lie to you?" Romano seemed to darken, and a moment later he started talking again. "Around here, he's the lord and master, and nothing happens without him knowing. He's like a king: he does whatever he wants and doesn't owe explanations to anybody."

"And don't people complain?"

"About what? But, besides, listen to me, there's no one around here with the courage to complain. It's dangerous; this place is full of snitches. I don't like it much, but it is what it is. I think it's better to get along with him; he's a guy who knows how to repay favors."

"And ask for payback, too, I suppose."

"Look at it this way: this town practically doesn't exist; we don't get any grants or partnerships. Nobody cares what happens in Las Casas. Did you know there was a provincial governor who didn't even know we existed? Incredible, isn't it? And the mayor comes from a long line of landlords, all bigshots like him; ha-ha, that was a joke—his properties go back at least four generations. This didn't start yesterday."

"What, exactly, didn't start yesterday?"

They had arrived at the pensión. Romano parked the Jeep by the door.

"Don't ask questions. Go to your room and wait. If there's anything to do, and if he thinks it's all right, it'll get done."

Álvaro got out of the car. It was 6 PM and still light out. He had a wicked impulse to go for a walk till night fell upon him, lost, but instead he entered the pensión.

2) THE LADY VANISHES

Fabiana was cooking a stew that could be smelled from the corridor. She hummed a tune along with the radio; it sounded strange. Álvaro tried to listen over the off-key voice and the fragrance of the sautéed onions. He thought he recognized Mozart, sharpened his ears, and Fabiana cackled a celestial chorus: the *Requiem*. He stood there with the key in his hand, standing before the door of his room, with a knot in his throat.

He opened the door, sat down on the bed, lit a cigarette with Alicia's Zippo. Ry Cooder had never sounded so far away. He thought about his film, about the two of them fleeing from the police while she complained about his unpreparedness. He should have filled the radiator; he knew that it had been leaking water. He hated himself and refused to think about this burden thrust upon him, no matter how hard he tried to escape it: They'd be in the cabin now, lying on a bearskin they had dreamed of for a whole year, wood burning in the fireplace, even if it was hot, naked, making love till they were happy and exhausted.

He looked at the camera. The night before—less than a day ago—it had worked fine till it turned off by itself with the two of them as the only protagonists of a typical porn flick in which she played the part of the innocent peasant girl with her curls dripping, and he was the slightly chubby devil dressed in red who possessed her till they couldn't move anymore. And it was all taped. He wanted to see Alicia; suddenly he was afraid he'd forget her face.

He turned on the camera and placed his eye in the viewfinder, saw the black-and-white image. There was the road; he noticed errors in the angles, liked certain shots, approved of the John Ford-style lighting. Alicia complained about the place and the lack of water, and her face became familiar once more. Now he moved in closer, announcing his intention of baptizing that aridity with his own sweat and the sweat of others: Woman, he had said, you're about to surrender to male dominance. And he had done his Dracula imitation. A cut, and the mirror in the room lit up; now there was the shower scene, strangely silent because the camera hadn't captured the audio very well. There she was, still indifferent to the eye that had spied on her soapy body. Then came another cut, because now the camera was turned off and he, someday, was going to tell her about his stealth recording. When she emerged from the bathroom wrapped in the white towel—her eyes gleaming after the shower and her skin looking lighter, her curls dripping—he could still smell that freshly-showered scent. He turned the camera back on and now he saw what he had recorded and remembered his playfully obscene remarks. Alicia, by way of reply, played the diva he always demanded of her: she ran through her entire repertoire of pouts for him, winked an eye, and became Marilyn as seen in a medium shot, waiting for the subway to go by so that her bouffant skirt would fly up to the sky; then came a close-up where she half-shut her magical lids like Greta Garbo, lit up the camera and regaled it with a wild, steamy gesture, imitating Rita Hayworth; now she sat down and was Marlene Dietrich, stealing the scene by crossing her perfect, endless legs as Álvaro closed the angle and backed up so that Ingrid Bergman, in an epiphany, would once more suffer Rick's farewell as the plane's engines revved up; a fade, and now she was reciting lines from *Ninotchka*, from *Casablanca*, from *Some Like it Hot*. For the finale, Alicia laughed, and the laughter echoed in his memory. Álvaro reached out a hand, without interrupting the filming; the hand entered the screen from the left; she gestured like an old-fashioned lady being stalked, took a step backward, bumped her back against the wall. Álvaro's hand grabbed the bath towel and tossed it aside, leaving a white, damp mark on the floor, to one side of the screen. She, the pure, Victorian lady, covered her breasts with her arms, and then the camera descended toward her pubic hair and parked there till Alicia's hand intervened again. Now he remembered: he had ordered her to open the chest and she had obeyed. He saw some damp, slightly moth-eaten rags emerge from the trunk. She looked at the camera, and as she pinched her nose, making a disgusted face, one breast peeked out lazily from behind something that might have been a blouse. Álvaro grew irritated and took a step toward her. This one, he ordered, put on this one, and "this one" was the peasant dress. Peasant girls are obedient; you give the orders, patrón, said the submissive Alicia. Do you want me to put on underwear, patrón? No! Álvaro roared in his abuser-of-schoolgirls voice; you'll be fine just like that. You're going to have an encounter with the devil, he explained, carefully depositing the camera on a shelf as he taped the shot in fish-eye, taking in the whole bed, the closed window, part of the room. The door wasn't included in the shot. It was enough: the party in the desert would be recorded. That's where he came into view: he pulled that diabolical monstrosity, with its trumpet missing, out of the chest, put it on with a complicit expression of disgust, stood in profile before the lens, and, on seeing the scene, took note of his bulging package, ready for some serious action. Alicia hadn't seen that, either, but she could follow the game to its conclusion—to that conclusion alone.

The viewfinder turned cloudy. Álvaro withdrew his eye, turned off the camera, and wiped his tears. Stupid bitch, he thought, where have you gone, he repeated quietly, as mute as his camera, always the same thing, I have to come and save you from your screw-ups, you're ridiculous, you've probably gone off with some wacko from the town, one of those guys you feel sorry for; the idiot's probably crying for his mama and drooling, I can see your Mother Teresa face, how your heart broke, what else, you took his hand and put it against your chest, and the monkey took you... where did he take you? Where did you go? Why do you do these things, you're so crazy, Alicia, I want to go home, please come back.

He closed his eyes and opened them again. He looked at his watch: it was almost twelve. Alicia wasn't there, and it was bad to go out at night: it's dangerous, the cruel mayor and his hesitant henchman had warned him. The smell of stew had dissipated but was still detectable. The camera rested next to his belly, between his bent knees and his chest. His left arm rested on it; the right arm held it up without effort. Alicia wasn't there; no, Alicia was never there, but now she wasn't there like never before, at that pensión, in that bed, beside him as she always and never was, and his stomach was a puncture wound, the turn of a screw, a feverish chill, a flame of fear and guilt: all the unreality of the world was concentrated there, on top of his belt, above his navel. The navel of the world: Alicia wasn't there, it was true; there was no turning back; she had gotten lost in the desert, holding hands with a demon. The fat guy was right: they should all be killed, useless puppets, happy-go-lucky dummies with their filthy pleasures. Right now they would be in the cabin down south, on top of the bearskin, naked.

3) A MAN WHO DOESN'T BELIEVE ANYMORE

El Tolo was downstairs. Álvaro had tried to sleep for a while, but finally gave up. The window in his room faced an empty lot, and he wasn't about to keep watching the video, so he decided to go downstairs to smoke and look out the window of the lobby. El Tolo was smoking, and when he heard footsteps, he turned his head.

"You can't sleep." The ember grew stronger, there was a sigh, and he was covered with a haze of smoke.

"I nodded off for a while, but now I'm wide awake. What about you?"

"I hardly sleep. Your car will be ready in two days. I've gotten all the parts—you were lucky."

"Man, am I lucky," said Álvaro and lit his cigarette. The Zippo's flame lit the room for a moment, revealing El Tolo's face looking at him.

"Come, sit down. Look at this."

Álvaro walked over and looked out the window. The avenue, just like the night before, was empty and yellow. They remained silent. A light breeze stirred the treetops; beyond them, the square was a wasteland, and farther still, the avenue plunged into the darkness. There was a squeak. Álvaro looked at El Tolo.

"It's the swings," the naval mechanic explained.

"What about the swings?"

"They move."

"It must be the wind."

"This isn't wind."

"And the trees?"

El Tolo didn't answer. He smoked and stared at the street.

The treetops whispered, and the squeak changed, fading and returning.

"A breeze is moving them, but that doesn't move the swings."

"So why do they move."

"Don't you know? Didn't they tell you anything? It's strange, don, around here people tell everything right away. They told you about the huemules, I imagine."

"They went away."

"That's what they say, but they're lying. You were at the mayor's house. Didn't you see anything?"

"I saw the heads mounted on the walls. I don't know why that matters."

"It depends. There are no huemules anymore. Just the heads you saw there. Before, there were more of them."

"And what happened to them?" The question was hardly more than an attempt at politeness.

"This is a town that loves to hunt."

"Why are you telling me all this? My wife's disappeared and you talk to me about deer and dogs."

Álvaro took a long drag, followed by another, coughed briefly, scratched his head and lowered his eyes. A silence fell. The two men sat there, staring at one another in the shadows, illuminated by the cigarette embers, quiet, as the dawn slipped in soundlessly. The treetops still whispered.

"You're right," said El Tolo after a while. He coughed and turned around to look at the empty street.

Álvaro stubbed out his cigarette and stood up. When his foot touched the first step, he stopped and said to the smoking shadow:

"What happened to the huemules?"

"They disappeared; there were too many of them. There never were regulations or a hunting season, and they all died off. Outside there are packs of wild dogs, did you know that? They kept them for hunting, and when there were no more hue-mules, they set them loose. They survived, like the wild beasts. They can be dangerous," El Tolo said, and his shadow shrugged.

Álvaro climbed two steps and stopped again.

"Does that happen a lot around here?"

"That animals disappear?"

"I'm talking about people; I don't care about your damn huemules."

"You *should* care. No, it's unusual for that to happen. Sometimes you'll see strange accidents, people lying on the road, cars that turned over on a straightaway."

The swing squeaked. The breeze let up for a moment and then resumed. There was a groan.

"What was that?"

"I told you, the swings. They're moving."

"Didn't you hear anything? Like a voice? I thought I heard someone moan."

"It's possible. You can hear things sometimes. And if you pay attention, you might see something, too. That's why you shouldn't go out."

"Look, Tolo, don't talk to me about ghosts. There must be someone out there."

"Who."

"I don't know. One of those Down kids."

"Sometimes they do go out, it's true. Poor things, they're like angels, but they don't understand anything."

At that moment a bang, clear and crisp, broke out, framed by the silence. Then the breeze picked up again, moving things around. And there was squeaking.

"See what I'm saying?" insisted El Tolo. "You shouldn't go out."

"And you never go out?"

"Not anymore. I used to be a believer, and I went out at night, too, but now I don't believe in anything."

"Please, tell me. You know something."

"About your missus? Don't believe everything you're told. I don't know what happened to her, but lots of things have happened here. How should I know if she has something to do with them? Are you sure you came here by accident? I'm asking because your car could have gone on just fine; it was a question of giving it enough water. You've really gotta be absent-minded to forget that. And the dashboard works perfectly, so you must have noticed."

"What are you saying? Never in my life would it have occurred to me to spend my vacation in this place; I didn't even know it existed till that old fucker Tanco showed up. The car broke down and was waiting there where you found it. I don't know what kind of mystery you're trying to find in that."

"Look, if that's the way it is, your missus might be, I don't know, somewhere. Better not to ask any more questions; it's a waste of time. Go to the hospital tomorrow and…"

"Yeah, I know, and to the police station, they told me that already," Álvaro interrupted.

"… and it would also be a good idea for you to go to the morgue," El Tolo went on. "To the police station too, for sure. They're the places where you go to look for people who've disappeared. Your wife had no papers, I heard. No one could recognize her, so if something did happen to her and she's wandering around, they must be waiting for you. Do that and stop worrying—huemules don't bite. Get some rest, don."

$\{VII\}$

CONFUTATIS

1) WILD DOGS

He began at the morgue, trying to confront his fears by facing the worst option first. He walked along the avenue to the town hall, asked for directions, and was told to turn the corner. The morgue was on the same block; in fact, it was the same building, they explained, but you entered through a back door made of oak. The gold-toned plaque read JUDICIAL MORTUARY; you couldn't miss it. His feet felt heavy, and even though he was still wearing his Nike Airs, he felt like he had on lead hiking boots. He was trembling, and he trembled even more when he turned the corner and saw the oak door. He knocked with a bronze knocker that hung to one side, above the sign. He knocked three times and waited, trembling all the while. He lit a cigarette, puffed away, looked around, trembled, and noticed, on the opposite sidewalk, kitty-cornered from him, a large, green metal door:

AGNUS DEI

HOME FOR CHILDREN WITH SPECIAL NEEDS

He knocked once more with the bronze knocker, and then he heard a voice:

"Hold on," the voice announced. "Just a minute, what's the big rush to come in here? I don't get it."

The door opened, revealing a middle-aged man, bald and very thin. He was wearing an apron of some synthetic material that had once been white and now was covered with black, dried blood and other traces of something that Álvaro preferred not to recognize. He wore loose-fitting, green rubber gloves—more appropriate for washing dishes—and his left hand held a scalpel of indeterminate colors on the tip and on the blade.

"What's up?" he asked. He didn't seem surprised; he had been waiting for him. His voice, Álvaro thought, was as screechy as last night's swings.

"Have we met?"

"At the bar, the other day—I was there watching them play truco when you walked in. Anyone could see you were nervous."

"You know what I'm here for."

"Yes, of course. I'm the eviscerator. That's my job. I'm a scientist, but here I do everything, on account of the budget cuts, you see. I'm not sure I'll be able to help you, but I've got a couple of Jane Does, and maybe, who knows, we might be able to clear up the situation a little. I have an idea who they are, but this thing is kind of hairy. Come in and I'll show you."

They entered, the bald man in front, with Álvaro following.

"Why is it hairy?"

"They're unrecognizable. What happened to them, those two women, is a disaster. They didn't leave a crumb. But it'll work out. I'm an optimist."

"So they're women?"

"Yes, and fairly young, between twenty and thirty, one of them, and as for the other one, we'll have to see. But somewhere in that range. They might have been neighbors, but since there's been no report yet, it's not definite. Sometimes things happen to people in the desert, and there they stay. Then someone brings them in, half-eaten by vermin, and it gets pretty fucked up trying to figure out who they are. I'd say in general they can be easily recognized, but with these, it's taking me longer than usual. Look, I know everybody, so I'm in charge of identifying the bodies, even though it's not my job, like I said; I do everything around here. And if I can't, someone always shows up. It must've been the wild dogs, for sure, dangerous beasties, they make work for the morgue. But with these two, they ate like boars, gnawing all the way down to the bone, you know; one of them is missing the lower maxillary; they ripped it right off. And the other one—they ate her whole forehead and one of the parietal bones is unworkable, if you get what I mean. What're you gonna do, it comes with the territory, like the explorer said."

"What happens to them?" asks Álvaro, feeling his stomach turn.

"Who?"

"Um... I don't know, to the women who spend the night in the desert... the dead ones."

"A flat tire, let's say; they don't know how to fix it and wait for their knight on a white horse to come along and solve their problem, and since he doesn't show up, they start walking. Anyway, vacations start when you leave home, right? Since you can't see the town from there, they get lost. There are stones everywhere, and sooner or later they take a misstep, and crack!—a broken ankle. Now it's a question of time. They sit down to rub the foot and wait; maybe the knight is still on his way, you know? By the time they figure out what's what, it's already night, and as you've probably noticed, around these parts, when it grows dark, it's freezing, see, and besides, the wild dogs are out there. But most of all, my friend, at this time of the night, no one goes outside, I mean no one, especially not into the desert; even the Pope himself couldn't get help. It's not so unusual, really—don't think it is—it happens pretty often, even to the locals, though they all know what the deal is. It could be that they just don't learn, so many dummies running around couldn't have come from a cabbage patch. And as far as outsiders are concerned, listen to me, it's a fact that one out of every four spends the night out there and in the morning they bring them to my office; these are the real statistics. What I don't get is why now there are more women than before; it must be modern times, they'll try everything and then they pay the consequences. A woman without her man shouldn't go anywhere. Well, here we are; we've arrived. See why it took me so long to let you in? It's far from the door, and I was working."

They proceeded to a room with white tiled walls. There were several metal tables with covered bodies. Álvaro saw them and stopped short.

"Take it easy, man," the bald guy said. "What you're looking for is in the freezer."

They turned down a corridor and entered a spacious room: in back was a warehouse refrigerator, its doors covered with a wood veneer and its motor on top. Their steps echoed.

"It's the most modern one we could get our hands on, but it works very well, eh?   Germany technology, the finest of all; I can keep a body here for months. Well, let's take a look."

The eviscerator opened the door, revealing two black bags, one next to the other, two human forms seated back to back; then he leaned over and began to open one of them.

"Wait a second," Álvaro said. "What happens if it's Alicia?"

"I don't know, man, you'll take her home. What do you want me to do? It's your wife."

"No, I… listen, not like that. Why don't you open it and tell me what you see?"

"You're not up to it?"

"No. I'm asking you, please. I can't."

The man opened the bag and peeked in.

"I don't know what to tell you. This one's the brunette. Could it be her? She's the one who's twenty-something."

"What else do you see."

"I'd have to take her out." He was looking at him. Álvaro insisted.

"Tell me what else you see. What's she wearing?"

"It's hard to tell. She's destroyed, you can imagine, two nights out in the weather and with those dogs: there's not much left."

The eviscerator manipulated, skittered around, dug, lifted unlikely parts.

"What do you see, goddammit? Just tell me that."

"This one's wearing a T-shirt, looks like, or a sweatshirt, I can't really say. It's in shreds."

There followed the sound of rubbing, shifting, squeaking of polyethylene, the tearing of fabric.

"What color?

"It looks light, but it's a huge mess—look how disgusting: dried blood, brain matter everywhere." He lifted a filthy hand and held it toward Álvaro.

"I can't."

"What do you mean, you can't? You've got to identify the body."

"I don't know if it's my wife," said Álvaro. "Maybe I should leave and come back later. I can't do this: if she's in the hospital and I'm wasting time with you—no, no, I'm going to look for her there." He turned around and started to walk away.

"Look, that's where we got her from, eh? Don't lose hope, maestro; you need a little patience."

Álvaro was moving away, and the man kept talking to him. He raised his voice: "It's a bad time, and that's that. You've gotta grow some balls, man; you're looking for your woman, what a chickenshit. Don't take too long, jefe, I'll wait for you till five. After that I'm closing up and heading home for a barbecue."

The slammed door silenced the eviscerator.

2) TURBULENCE IS THE RESULT OF ALL THOUGHT

He passed the green door with the sign that read AGNUS DEI HOME FOR CHILDREN WITH SPECIAL NEEDS. There were the mayor's Down Syndrome children. He stopped for a moment, and without giving it much thought, crossed and rang the bell. The chatter of voices rang out, guttural sounds, a pathetic, childlike uproar that grew louder when the doorbell rang. Álvaro withdrew, sprinted to the corner, and hid behind a walnut tree.

A few seconds later the door opened and a nun's head, covered by a headdress with a peaked coif, emerged; her face wasn't visible. Her head turned, first from right to left and then right again, but she didn't see Álvaro behind the walnut tree. The door closed. Something made him decide to head for the church. Inside, people were praying; to one side of the nave, a woman standing at a microphone droned out a psalm in Latin. The parishioners responded "Amen." The priest couldn't be seen. Álvaro explored the side aisles and stopped before an image of the Virgin. A woman with a white scarf on her head prayed, kneeling. Farther along, on a tumulus bordered with Baroque molding, rested a slightly pompous sarcophagus containing the body of a bishop: *JEAN DUPREE*, read a marble plaque adorned with fresh flowers and the dates 1713–1796. BENEDICTUS TU ERES said the gilded letters in bas-relief.

A woman in a wheelchair studied the sarcophagus and whispered.

A silence fell after the last Amen and there was a murmur: the priest was about to enter. Álvaro sat on a bench and watched the man: vigorous, with an authoritative air, in a black cassock, old and gray-haired. Álvaro saw him accept the microphone, which the woman reverently extended toward him. Without preliminaries, he raised one palm toward the faithful and began to speak:

"Confutatis maledictis," he warned.

The air had frozen. His palm closed up, turning into a fist, crowned by a cautionary finger.

"Flamis acribus addictis." The finger pointed toward heaven, then toward the inferno.

"Voca me cum benedictis." Now he opened his generous arms and gave way to hope.

"Amen," echoed throughout.

"Oro supplex et acclinis." Prostrate and supplicating.

"Cor contritum quasi cinis: Gere curam mei finis." Because the hour had arrived and it was the moment of contrition.

"Amen," echoed throughout.

Another silence fell. At the back of the church there was a gentle noise that resounded briefly and clearly and then suddenly hushed; a few pigeons flew under the cupola. The priest kept his gaze fixed on the people, the suspense grew tighter, the microphone amplified his breathing.

"Offertorium," he announced. "Let us pray."

Domine Jesus Christe, Rex gloriae
Libera animas omnium fidelius defunctorum
De poenis inferni et de profundo lacu.

The old man's voice grew stronger and more severe. He fixed his gaze on the eyes of the people. He seemed to be speaking to them one by one. Enraptured, perhaps fearful of the wrath of the Lord embodied in that imposing cleric, they continued praying fervently:

Libera eas de ore leonis
Ne absorbeat eas tartarus, ne cadant in obscurum
Sed signifer sanctus Michael
Repraesentet eas in lucem sanctam
Quam olim Abrahae promisisti et semini ejus.

He grew silent again and once more the pigeons fluttered overhead. A woman sitting beside Álvaro wept soundlessly as her tears continued to fall. The man's voice thundered mercilessly.

He seemed furious:

> *Hostias et preces, tibi, Domine, laudis offerimus*
> *Tu suscipe pro animabus illis, quadem hodie*
> *memoriam facimus*
> *fac eas, Domine, de morte transire ad vitam*
> *Quam olim Abrahae promisisti et semini ejus.*

Then, nothing, barely a trace of his breath pulsing faster behind the microphone and echoing throughout the entire church.

"Amen," he said a moment later.

"Amen," replied the congregation in a single voice.

"No one gets out of here alive," the priest began, and the hair rose on Álvaro's back.

"There will be no salvation without Jesus," he admonished, "because that's how it is: no one gets out of here alive. The dead will not arise till Judgment Day, and only then will there be bugles in heaven, and a great pit will open for the unholy to fall into. But no one gets out of here alive. And we are all in the hands of our Lord Jesus Christ; we must remember that: only with Him is there salvation. Whoever strays from His path will sow discord and will fall hopelessly. To be cleansed of our sins is our hope, our only hope. It's as simple and pure as when it was written in the Holy Gospel. We must accept the fact that God appears on mysterious paths and that He doesn't have to speak clearly. And when the voice of God rings out, it thunders throughout the universe for those who know how to listen carefully. And I have listened to sinners, to usurers, to the Pharisees who greedily exchange their merchandise before the temple, the excess evidence of the pleasures that only money can buy. Heaven will belong to the humble, it has been said, and it is true, but be careful: Humility before God means knowing, even though we may have power, land, and riches, that nothing, absolutely nothing can be compared to Him, because nothing is worth as much as His beautiful and indivisible visage. We shall see who can bear the Lord's gaze when the time comes. Because, my brothers, my children, my flock, He created us in His image and likeness, and He did not make us in any other way. He didn't make us terrible or treacherous; He didn't give us horns, because those were for His Fallen Angels, may God keep him forever in His dark dwelling place. He didn't give us three eyes or four hands. No, God gave us understanding and a place, now on earth, for us to live in and have a house and bread, and later, there, beside His throne, which will be our last, final place. Did I say 'understanding?' Be careful. Turbulence is the result of all thought. That is why no one gets out of here alive. Because when we think, we make mistakes, we lose our way, we are at the mercy of the mobs, because only God's thought will lead us to safe harbor. He, who is all mercy and love, teaches us to think properly, tells us the Truth that is Absolute and admits no other opinion or dissent. There is no argument in the Word of the Lord, only obedience and contrition. Who is so proud as to raise his voice to doubt the Holy Word? Upon him curses will fall, his will be the place reserved for those who choose darkness over eternal light. And for the others, those lambs of God, there will be eternal light and glory."

"Amen," said the lambs of God, and there was an intense silence.

Then the priest continued his sermon:

"Let us become worthy of His grace; let us cleanse our home; let us not allow the dissolution of our purest values, because that is the precise, unrecoverable beginning of all sins. Today is a day like any other, that is, an exceptional day, one that will never return. Never, ever will this hour or this light or this gathering in this sacred house return. There will be others, true, but never again this precise, precious day. So I ask you, have we complied with the Word of the Lord? Will we lose this divine, unique opportunity to be by His side? It is always a good time for redemption, but in the end, our sins will weigh heavily."

The priest gestured, signaling the end of his sermon. Then, in a single, respectful, orderly body, the faithful passed to the confessionals. That would take a while, and then they would return, kneel, receive the Body of Jesus, and finally they would be blessed.

No one gets out of here alive, the priest had said.

Álvaro felt dizzy. He needed air.

3) AT THE SERVICE OF THE COMMUNITY

The sun beat down on the square, illuminating the sandbox, overwhelming the parishioners, driving the pedestrians away. A scrawny dog panted, lying in the shade of a tree. Álvaro, who was heading straight toward it, suddenly saw it and stopped short a few feet away; the dog lifted its head and watched him for a moment, then decided to return to its nap. To avoid getting closer, Álvaro took a detour behind the motionless swings. He crossed the square and entered the police station, right next to the movie theater. He introduced himself to the officer on duty and asked to see the Chief of Police. He had come at the behest of the mayor, he explained. The officer looked at him, clearly annoyed by the heat, but with a phony expression of interest that didn't conceal the fact that he was dealing with yet more crap on a miserable day like this. He made Álvaro wait for a moment while he ducked into an office in back. When the officer opened the door, Álvaro managed to catch a glimpse of the Chief. He heard comments, questions, and he thought there might have been an expression of vexation. After a while, the door opened again.

The Chief of Police, predictably, was obese, though less so than the mayor. He was sitting behind his desk, sweating and panting. Off to one side, a steel fan blew, ruffling some papers that were held down by a glass ashtray.

"How can I help you?" asked the Chief, who had a little sign on his desk that said: INSP./ COMMISSIONER JORGE AYALA.

"I don't know if you've been informed of my situation. You

may have heard that I… we're tourists… but anyway… do you know what I'm talking about?"

"You can't find your wife, I found out about it today. When did she disappear?"

"I don't know if she disappeared; she might have gotten lost and maybe she's got amnesia, I don't know… something, a blow on the head. She's very absent-minded, and if she's not with me, she gets lost easily. This is what happened yesterday morning: I woke up and she wasn't there anymore. Something must've happened to her during the night or in the early morning, I couldn't say, I didn't hear anything; I was very tired and I slept like a log."

"Okay, I understand. As you can imagine, I need to ask you a few questions; it could be uncomfortable, but I have no choice. All right? Tell me, sir, is it like her to do these things? Is she in the habit of leaving home, shall we say, late at night? You get what I mean? I'm asking if she's… well, liberal, with independent habits, you know? You folks are from Buenos Aires; you have different customs there."

"No," replied Álvaro, feeling rage light up his face.

"Hmm. I understand. You have complete confidence in her. Look, when it comes to women, you can't take your eyes off them. I'm telling you because I know the score. Did you know that about a mile from here, along the back road, there's another hotel? And it's better than the Seagull, I can tell you that. That's where housewives go in the morning with their shopping bags under their arms. And not with their husbands, if you get what I mean. And that's not even counting the schoolgirls who show up in their uniforms and all. I can't even begin to tell you how many little whores there are around here. The parents go off to work, happy-go-lucky, thinking their daughters are at school. It's no crime: we know this because we're the police, but these things are rarely serious. Sure, there's a grove in front that can hide anyone, it's more discreet. The Seagull is visible to half the town; it's not a great place if what you want is a little privacy."

"My wife doesn't do things like that," Álvaro replied,

controlling his tone of voice. He looked at the Chief, who was sweating, and felt like he could wring his neck.

"Ah," said Ayala. He stood there, lost in thought; you could tell that he, too, didn't give a damn about Álvaro's story. He drummed his fingers on the desk, sweated a while; the fan rattled the papers, which didn't succumb, thanks to the glass ashtray. At last he asked: "So tell me, in complete confidence, does she take drugs? Maybe she was at home, and then..."

Álvaro exploded:

"Listen! I've come here for help, and you're trying to convince me that my wife is the only one responsible for this, that she's a hooker or a druggie—what the hell do you want? Are you going to help me, or are you going to keep up this bullshit?"

"Bullshit, you say." Ayala's eyes grew even colder, as if that were possible. "I'm sorry to give you such a bad impression, but you should know that this is what our work is all about. I can't dispatch men to investigate something that might not warrant investigation. Here in Las Casas nobody gets lost; if she's not here, there's got to be a reason for it, and I don't see why that reason can't be any of the ones I mentioned to you, which is what we find in most cases."

"Because"—Álvaro pondered what he was going to say and continued talking—"because neither my wife nor I live in Las Casas. And your case studies don't mean a damn thing to me; I know who I live with and what she's capable of doing. If this is all I can expect from the police, tell me now and I'll go look for help somewhere else."

"In any case, there are still some steps to be taken before she can be declared officially missing. One is the hospital and the other is the official declaration. When everything's in order, we'll go out looking for her. There's not too much to dig into. We'll organize a formal search, with dogs, and if necessary, the townspeople will put their shoulders to the wheel. I can't promise you results, as you surely understand, and, to be frank, I'm not so sure you've answered my questions. Women can surprise even the sharpest guy. And if she doesn't turn up, who knows, maybe she got involved in something she shouldn't have—this place isn't heaven. And the police do what they can, but with the budget cuts, I don't even have enough for air conditioning, you know?"

Commissioner Ayala took out a handkerchief, mopped his forehead, sighed, and poured himself a glass of water. As he brought it to his mouth, he raised his eyes toward Álvaro and offered him some. Álvaro shook his head no and waited for him to finish drinking.

"Meanwhile," the Chief went on, water dripping from the corners of his mouth and dampening his chubby cheeks, where the stubble of a few days' worth of beard had sprouted, "go to the hospital and ask for the director, who's a friend of mine. If your wife had an accident, it's better to start there." He dried his mouth with his hand; he had fat fingers and dirty fingernails. "But first talk to the clerk who'll take down your declaration. Let me warn you, though: if you file the declaration and for some reason you need to return home, every time your presence is required, you'll have to appear before the judge right here, no matter where you live"—he snorted—"so it would be a good idea for you to see a lawyer."

4) GO SEE THE WOMAN WITH THE HEAD

Álvaro sat down on a bench in the square and tried to think. He was getting embroiled in a bureaucratic tangle; he hadn't come looking for red tape or fat guys with dirty nails, and now he had to find a lawyer. He looked at the business card the Chief had handed him: DR. ABELARDO NOSEDA MARTÍNEZ, CRIMINAL DEFENSE ATTORNEY, it said, along with a phone number. The clerk had taken down his complaint with his expressionless, bored face, but he had committed an unexpected act of kindness toward the end: he recommended that attorney, he said, with a gesture of always complying with the law, because he was the best, as well as the only one in town, not counting a certain Laureano Casero, an old crook and drug addict who was only good for getting people into messes and taking their money.

Besides, he was nearly retired, so Noseda Martínez was the best option. And so Álvaro walked out of the police station, lit a cigarette, and crossed the square to sit down on a bench and think.

An old man sat down beside him. He smelled bad, and his appearance didn't seem appropriate for the climate: a dirty trench coat, brown, wrinkled suit, white socks, unpolished buttoned shoes, disheveled hair, a shirt that hadn't been changed in several days, and a badly knotted tie. He set down a student book bag between them, stretched out his legs, and stared blankly ahead. Álvaro moved away.

"I'm the one you're looking for," the old man blurted out.

"Excuse me?"

"Don't talk to Noseda; things will only get worse for you. He's involved in all that shady business. I'm the one you want."

"Who are you?"

"Dr. Laureano Casero, attorney, crook, and drug addict, as the sober guardians of the law must have already informed you. It's a relief to have a police force like that." He continued to stare straight ahead. "And don't bother going to the hospital; I've been there already and there's nothing going on. Have you got a cigarette?"

Álvaro held the box out and offered him a light.

"Why did your wife go out that night?"

"I don't know; I wasn't aware of a thing. If they saw her in the bar when she went downstairs for breakfast, where do you get the idea she went out at night?"

"I don't believe a word of what those guys in the bar said. Whatever they say, it's better to believe the opposite. She wasn't in the room, and it's unlikely anything happened to her in the daytime. It happens sometimes, but it's not typical. So, unless you have some brilliant inspiration, I don't see many possibilities."

"She might've gone downstairs for a smoke. She didn't like to smoke in the room," Álvaro mused, as if following the old guy's train of thought.

"She *doesn't* like," the lawyer chided him. "Don't kill her off just yet. Okay, she left the room and went downstairs for a smoke. Could she have gone out into the street?"

"It was cold; I don't think she…"

"And what if she saw something and got involved where she shouldn't have?" Casero interrupted him.

"Could be—the Chief of Police asked me the same thing, and truth is, that's what she's like: kind of a justice warrior. She always sticks her nose where it doesn't belong. But what could she have seen?"

"I'm starting to like this. A justice warrior, eh? We hardly know one another and already we're making progress. Look," Casero furtively slipped him a business card. "Call me at this number and we'll go on with this. It's not good for our health to keep talking here."

"Is the heat bothering you? Let's go to the bar across the way, I'll buy you a beer, and we'll be cooler," Álvaro offered. The lawyer looked at him.

"Don't be an idiot. Call me at this number today at five. And go to Agnus Dei, ask for Mother Aurora. That one has a head on her—hah! She'll clear up some things for you. I'm leaving now; you wait five minutes and then go." Casero stood up and started walking slowly. He had a limp. One shoe had a lift to even out his gait.

5) THE CLAMOR OF SIMPLE SOULS

Five minutes later, Álvaro set out toward the Home, walked around the block, and rang the bell again. This time he waited to be admitted while the same hair-raising shouts filled the air. A nun—perhaps the same one as before—appeared, in the same headdress and peaked coif that obscured her face. He introduced himself, mentioning Casero's name, and asked for Mother Aurora. He had to wait a moment, during which time he saw the Chief pass by in a police car, cross the side street and keep on going. He felt uneasy, though he didn't think the other man had seen him. He checked his watch: 12:00. He had the feeling he'd been ringing doorbells longer than that. The door opened and the nun invited him in.

"Mother Aurora will see you now. Follow me," she said and began walking ahead of him nervously, head down.

They walked down corridors, hearing strange voices that murmured behind the closed doors. At last they emerged onto a spacious patio which all the rooms faced. Álvaro could detect shadows behind the dirty windowpanes, multicolored figures, odd, eager, laughing faces that pushed one another aside to catch a glimpse of the visitor. The nun kept walking, never slowing her pace. They reached a staircase and climbed three floors. On the third floor they entered a large hall whose walls were covered with religious imagery. A Jesus with penetrating eyes stared at them from a painting as soon as they walked in and didn't take His eyes off them until they left His field of vision. Farther on, Saint George was slaying the dragon, followed by Mary nursing her Child, with Saint Anne watching over both. A large mural to the right warned of the destiny of souls in hell: horrific pain, eternal flames, hideous punishments falling upon the sinners, as the nun in the peaked headdress summoned all her energy to get away from Álvaro, who dawdled, contemplating the images. To him they looked crude, lacking in depth, amateurish. He recognized familiar faces: Che Guevara, Fidel Castro, Mao, mixed with other, anonymous, faces, all of them seemingly assaulted by demons whose exaggerated repugnance made them seem pathetic: sporting the customary long horns and inevitable goat's hooves, they drooled profusely and laughed, displaying oversized teeth, and slanted, squinty, crossed eyes that stared wildly; their heads were too small or too large; some bore humps; all of them laughed with their twisted mouths and dangling tongues as they launched unfortunate blasts of flatulence into the faces of famous communists and tore into their stomachs with their tridents. Behind them, tall and powerful, Satan, a sort of lunatic Buddha, lord and master of the fate of the wayward, approved with a beastly gesture and a voluminous belly.

They arrived at a large double door, where the nun stopped. She knocked with a minuscule fist that peeked out of her gray sleeve, and, when no one replied, she opened it. They entered a large, poorly-lit room, seemingly unoccupied.

The nun pointed to a chair and silently withdrew. Álvaro sat down, not knowing if he was alone. He tried to see, but the lack of light confused him; when he got used to the darkness, he was able to make out details. Close to the curtain, a seated woman silently observed him. She was a strange figure, he noted, her body disproportionate. She looked small to him, and only her ghostly head moved, framed by the white headdress. Barely a hint of a face, no movement, and she was watching him. Álvaro waited, swallowed. The seated woman was merely a head, and as his gaze grew clearer, she seemed to grow in her odd wheelchair. She was, in fact, something more than a face, but not much more: the slight body of an old doll, a snippet of a thing that ended on either side in a pair of impossibly small hands, with a torso like that of a magpie, and invisible legs that were lost among the unnecessary layers of her habit. Forever motionless and suspended by an orthopedic device that held her up by the neck, Mother Aurora seemed to be waiting for Álvaro to grow accustomed to the strangeness.

"Good afternoon," said the head. "How may I help you?"

"I don't know why I'm here, señora; the lawyer..."

"I'd prefer to be called Mother, if you don't mind; it's what people have called me for as long as I can remember."

"Sorry, of course, Mother," Alvaro began. "Casero—that's the lawyer's name, right?—seems to respect your judgment. He told me to come here and ask you about my wife. You may have heard that she's been missing since yesterday; everybody here knows it. Even Casero'd heard about it, but I hardly know him. I don't want to waste your time, but I'm getting desperate, and so far he seemed to me like the only friendly person in this place."

The woman listened attentively, and he didn't stop.

"She—her name is Alicia—slept with me night before last, and I don't know what happened, but when I woke up, she wasn't there anymore. I don't have any news about her, I'm scared and alone. Casero thinks that she must have gone out early that morning and maybe she saw something she shouldn't have seen, but things haven't gotten much farther than that. He also says that you know things, but he didn't explain what he was referring to because he left in a hurry. He seemed frightened. I've spoken to the mayor and the Chief of Police, but they'd rather think she left by herself or was involved in something fishy. My wife would never do a thing like that, and she doesn't do drugs, either. I don't understand how a person can disappear and they can take it so casually. I also went to the morgue, but I couldn't look at the bodies. Then I thought maybe the priest could help me, but today he gave a sermon that seemed like it was... from another era. Nobody gets out of here alive, that's what he said; how can he talk that way? It made my hair stand on end, so I left the church without asking him anything. Casero blew off the idea of going to the hospital; he inquired there himself and says that Alicia wasn't there. The police warned me not to trust him, but they didn't seem too reliable to me, either. I don't know where to go anymore, Mother."

"What you say about Casero surprises me. Your wife might have been in the hospital, but that doesn't mean they were about to tell him, with that reputation of his. People say that in a small town, people know everything, but this place is a cloistered convent, and very little filters in here. The fact that you've gotten in at all is strictly because of Casero; in spite of the fact that he's a worldly—or should I say somewhat immoral?—man, he's well received, so I was interested in your visit. The doorbell hardly ever rings in this place. Strangely, it's rung twice this morning. We know nothing about your wife."

Álvaro listened and stood up to leave.

"Wait, don't go yet. You know more about me than I know about you. You haven't even told me your name."

"You're right, excuse me. My name is Álvaro."

"Your first name is enough," Mother Aurora interrupted. "Keep your surname for your children, Álvaro. I don't know what might have happened to her. Here we deal with special needs children. Haven't you seen any since you arrived?"

"They asked me the same question. I didn't really notice. I saw some people who looked... different—the mayor, for example."

"Dupree."

"What?"

"His last name is Dupree. It's French."

"Dupree... it sounds familiar, but I don't know from where. He didn't introduce himself, but he talked about his ancestors. It seems he's descended from several generations in the town, according to Romano."

"Romano? Watch out for that man: all that remorse is suspicious."

"What are you talking about?"

"It's a confusing game that loosens naïve tongues. It's possible he may feel regret, but he's always right at Dupree's side, so it's best to be discreet when you're with that man. I've known him since he was a choir boy. You know, my world has always been the Church. As you can see, I'm wheelchair bound and paralyzed. I was born this way and will remain this way till the end. I have no control over any part of my body; the only things that move do it of their own accord. My heart doesn't ask permission to beat, and the same goes for my lungs, and that's enough."

Mother Aurora paused, sighed, and went on: "It's not that I imagine my personal story will be of interest to you, but I suppose I've seen things that could help you get your bearings. The only thing I have are my thoughts, and thinking is what I've been able to do throughout my whole life. I have five university degrees that I won't bore you with; I'm also a theologian and I speak thirteen languages, including some indigenous dialects, pleasures that one can indulge in when there's nothing else one can do. Perhaps that's why I run this place. It's by Papal recommendation, you know, which fills me with pride. The Lord knows why He gave me this destiny. As for me, the only thing that matters is to take care of my children in the best possible way. But sometimes they don't let me; it's not always possible to fulfill such a basic mission. I'm going to tell you a little story, and I hope you'll be able to appreciate it. It's a tradition that belongs to this town, the kind it's not so simple to get away from. Traditions start with the founding of a town and are preserved, against all the logic of modern times. That surname, Dupree, has existed in Los Huemules for many generations, even longer than Romano knows. A strange family. The first Dupree, whose name was Jean, came here from Basel, when there was nothing here but a couple of houses, and it's possible that's why the town has that name, Las Casas. I don't know if it's a family tradition or a strange kind of oblivion. A flamboyant type, devoted to demonology. A crazy man, if you ask me, but in those days—I'm talking about seventeen-sixty, more or less—things weren't like they are now. The Holy Office of the Inquisition was still around, and that fact adds important information. Just the same, I think he was as crazy as a goat. He wrote a book, *De Verum Naturae* is its short title; a copy of it is in the church library, an incunabulum, you understand, and not because it's a great book. This Dupree fellow had calculated the number of demons that inhabit hell, though his source remains a mystery. He claimed to have learned all that through a revelation; in short, it seems that in those days, angels came down to earth more often than they do now, and through visions, they possessed certain people who were headed for heaven or hell, and that's how they became famous and powerful. Dupree explained all that in a rather grandiose way, I think, perhaps because his visions wouldn't leave him alone, so he scattered his seed: monstrous, fallen angels, living among God's creatures, running into them every day in the streets, in their rooms, in their prayers, and their private moments, hurting them, stealing their souls, because the presence of those bogeymen was a sign that Satan wasn't satisfied. You know that Satan takes many different forms; his favorite way is through deception. He loves to appear with an angel's face, because he suffers from nostalgia, and he hides his true skin underneath. What is demonic, Dupree says, is to show a disagreeable face while feigning mercy, loving what is horrifying, believing it to be part of God. And people didn't see the truth in those hideous faces because of a kind of blindness they needed to be cured of. He was cured and wrote down the remedy. I've read it with a good deal of interest, you know. Inside those demons there's something attractive; they're like members of the family. I can give you the exact number: there are seven princes plus 7,405,926 devils in 1111 legions made up of 6666 infernal abortions. Do the math—it's simple. Dupree names the devils as if he had been down there, dining with Asmodeus; he describes them with remarkable precision: Ganga Gramma has four arms; the body of Eurinomos, prince of death, is crossed with countless wounds; Leonardo, grandmaster of orgies, has three horns and two faces, one of them on his backside, and fox's ears. And the Great Duke Astaroth, treasurer of hell, can be recognized by his unbearable stench. The descriptions continue in the same vein and return somewhat repetitively, in a treatise of nearly a thousand pages. Dupree was a priest, but he left offspring; these things happen.

Father Dupree, whom you met this morning, is one of his descendants. The mayor is his brother. But God works in mysterious ways. There's a son, right here, in my Home. They say he's the mayor's son, but—and maybe this is what Casero meant—around here we know things that no one should know. I'm doing you no favors by telling you all this; it could be dangerous, but I suppose you need to know."

"I don't know what this story has to do with my wife."

"Maybe nothing, but frankly I doubt that. Shall I go on?"

"Please do."

"The child belongs to Father Dupree, not at all surprising if you think of his ancestor, but, as we know, a priest is free to pull the strings on which the lives of his faithful depend, but not to make babies and let them graze wherever they want. And so he gave this son the backing of all his power; he protects him, but he doesn't acknowledge him in public, which means that everybody knows it, even though that's no reason for them to know so much, if you follow my drift. This son is an open secret. Everybody knows he exists; most people have seen him in photos, and the closest to him have met him in person. All of them, without exception, know that the boy is here and that his real father never comes to visit him. The mayor decided to do something about that; he entered him in the records as his own child, while at the same time taking him out of circulation. And it so happens that those monsters, as the townspeople gleefully call them, carry the burden of a dark history that comes from the first Dupree. So vivid were his descriptions, so insistently did he conjure the horrid images of demons in his sermons, that you can imagine the destiny of any malformed child who showed up in this town."

"I still don't understand the connection to my wife. What happened? They hid them, I suppose; that must have been how this home got started."

"They hunted them." Mother Aurora paused and Álvaro looked up. "Dupree came from Europe, he had taken part in the Inquisition trials, and here he established his own town, his flock, as he said. From the day he had his first congregation, he spoke to them of his experiences. That's how he described them, as experiences; he didn't call them celestial visions, but rather he told of events he claimed to have attended in person, both of the Inquisition and of hell—he made no distinction. He had been to both places, so why bother clarifying the meaning of some metaphor, if indeed there was any. Perhaps he was sincere and for him there were no differences, or, shall we say, perhaps he could defend this thesis theologically: it is impossible to establish a difference between what the human eye sees—and only God determines what can be seen—and what the eye of God Himself sees and describes to the mystic. For example, what kind of creatures live in hell, what are they like, what are their functions, the hierarchies, the chain of command? I suppose it must have been a sort of divine census of all of creation, an account presented to the inquisitor, who then redoubled his efforts to fight whatever was un-Christian, that is to say, demonic. Whatever is outside of God belongs only to the devil. The effect it had on people was phenomenal; it unleashed a paranoia that seemed less crazy in those days than it sounds now, although I imagine that could happen at any time and in any place. A witch hunt, it's called; you're probably familiar with the term. The first cases were fierce: in the beginning, the guard acted alone, but later the townspeople joined in. If the demons were those figures who horrified the sensitive souls of the era, and if, at the same time, they presented themselves as the harmless creatures they were, that discrepancy could be explained only by the trickery of Satan. You surely know about the witchcraft trials: they chained the accused and threw her into the water; if she floated, it confirmed that the accusation was justified, and then they sent her to the bonfire. If she drowned, her innocence was proved and her soul was saved. That same logic prevailed here: they organized, burst into homes, yanked the deformed people out by the hair, even newborns. No one could escape the flames. A little, home-grown Crusade. And, of course, they burned the houses down and took off with all they could carry. It was a war, and they took things as their well-deserved plunder. God's Heroes, they demanded to be called. God's Warriors was another name they used. Many traditional fortunes grew out of this. Dupree himself led countless violent attacks of the same ilk. You can see his tomb in the church. *Benedictus tu eres*, the plaque says; it's a theological injustice, a true cosmic error, to bless that monster. Things like that plant roots, they leave traces that transcend history. I'm thirsty. Would you be good enough to hand me that cup?"

Álvaro put the metal straw in her mouth, and the nun drank. A silence fell. Mother Aurora was upset.

"But that doesn't happen anymore?" Álvaro ventured, intuiting a connection.

"This town seems cursed; deformed people are born here. I don't know if that has an explanation; it seems like destiny's revenge—for all those they killed, more were born. You can see it for yourself: I didn't manage to be an exception, and yet here I am. Nothing ever happened to me. But sometimes things do happen. There are plenty of people who think that war never ended. Dupree is a revered name around here, and if anyone found out what we've been talking about, there's no guarantee I'd come out of it in one piece, even if I had the support of the Pope himself."

"Who are the ones who do that?"

"The powerful, of course. It's not so different from those long-ago times."

"But you're talking to me about local politics. And with all due respect, Mother, and far be it from me to underestimate you, it sounds a little fantastic. Who, today, is going to believe that... mumbo-jumbo? Your Home is the best proof that today people tolerate what used to be demonized."

There was a brief silence and what followed was a controlled outburst.

"You *are* underestimating me," the nun roared. "And you believe that people everywhere think alike. In Los Huemules you may find that the same person who connects to the Internet also goes out into the street and is capable of kicking a Down Syndrome child who crosses in front of him. And that saintly gentleman harbors no doubt that he's just committed an act to benefit humanity. Look, I don't know why so many deformed people are born here; really, there's no explanation. Maybe their blood is hopelessly contaminated, God only knows. Terrible things happen in this town. They even come and kidnap my students so that they can hunt them down at night. And it's not something I know because they've told me about it; their job is to keep me out of the loop."

"What are you telling me, Mother?" asked Álvaro, shocked.

"They hunt them like huemules, that's what I'm telling you, with shotguns, with pistols. Then they leave them in the desert, and there they stay, dead or alive, at the mercy of God and the wild dogs. Nobody asks questions, and it goes on. It's a tradition, like so many others, that starts out one way and becomes eternalized in another. No one literally eats the body of Christ, but the idea is quite cannibalistic, if you think about it for a moment. I have no way of stopping this brutality, nor can I prevent anyone from delivering their prey to them from this place. I don't know who does it; lots of nuns work here. You don't believe me? I have no reason to make this up. Here I am, trapped forever. Do you understand? I'm just a head, and that's what I work with. I oversee the Home with the help of my secretary; I can teach master's level classes in pre-Socratic philosophy; I'm fluent in Latin and ancient Greek; Hebrew is like my native language; I recite poetry in Aramaic; and I would be well qualified to read the Rosetta Stone, but whichever nun's on duty has to wipe my ass. Is that clear? I've talked too much, considering that you're a stranger. Please, press that button, and someone will come and see you out."

{VIII}
LACRIMOSA

ÁLAVARO'S STOMACH WAS a rock as he walked beneath the sun, and from the rock came tremors that snaked down his back and extended to his arms. It was hard to breathe, feeling that his back trembled of its own accord. A few cars passed by like ovens overcome by the heat and aridity of the atmosphere; they pulled away, crawling along the avenue. Ayala and Romano were on the corner where the Home stood, whispering. When they saw Álvaro, they fell silent. Romano turned toward him for a moment, then continued chatting with the Chief of Police. Álvaro continued on his way to the pensión and crossed the square. The dog still snoozed in the shade; the parishioners, who were still drinking gin, watched Álvaro go by. He crossed diagonally. Tanco passed by on his bicycle, and Álvaro thought he would stop when their paths met, but the man averted his glance and kept pedaling.

He crossed the avenue, walked two blocks, and on a side street recognized the tail fins of his coupe sticking out of El Tolo's garage. The car was dismantled, and from underneath protruded the legs of the mechanic, who was humming a tango. Álvaro walked into the shop.

"Who's there?" asked El Tolo, continuing to work.

"It's me, Álvaro—I've come to look for some things. Will you be much longer?"

El Tolo was resting on a platform supported by ball bearings. With a push he went flying out from underneath.

"What do you say, Álvaro—it'll be ready tomorrow."

Álvaro opened the trunk and started rifling through his bags.

"Any news?"

"No. I talked to everyone, seems like, and here I am. I even spoke to Mother Aurora, the one from the orphanage."

"You talked to her?" El Tolo's expression didn't reveal much more than surprise, but his question made Álvaro feel uneasy.

"Did I do something wrong?"

"Nah, you never know." El Tolo started to stand up; he had a wrench in his right hand and grease on his face.

"Look, Álvaro, I don't like this. I think you're asking too many questions, and I don't know where they're gonna lead you. Honestly, I'd recommend that you leave town. I can give you a hand: I'll lend you my truck and you can go to Arizmendi, it's around sixty miles south of here, set yourself up there, and wait. Tomorrow I'll head out there with your car, return it to you, and you can go back home. When you're far away you'll be able to do things better than you would here, all alone and with no idea what this is all about."

Álvaro glowered at him with hatred.

"Do I look like a chickenshit to you? You think I'm going to take off just like that, with no news about my wife? No, look, what I'm gonna do is be a real pain in the ass. I'm gonna break some balls till they give me an answer that make sense. It's impossible that nobody knows anything. I don't know what kind of shit goes on in this place, and I'm not interested in finding out, but I'm not giving up so easily."

He had a bag in his hand and he shook it in front of El Tolo, who had by now reached a standing position.

"Is there a phone at the pensión?

"Who you gonna call?"

"It's none of your business. Will you let me use it?"

"Talk to my missus," El Tolo replied and slipped beneath the car again.

Álvaro left and walked toward the pensión. When he arrived, he saw the police car pull away and turn the corner; the clerk was driving. He entered. There was no aroma of stew. He called out, but Fabiana didn't answer. A dog barked in the distance. He found the telephone, but it had a lock on it. He checked the time: it was still a while till 5:00.

He walked into his room and realized that someone had been there. The clerk had just turned the corner. Nothing was missing, no one had disturbed his things, everything seemed to be in order, but someone had come in, and it wasn't Fabiana. The video camera was in a different position, on top of the bed, just where he had left it, in its case, where he always kept it, but the case had been left unlocked, something he never did. He turned it on: they had been watching. There were the two of them, making love; the devil costume had fallen next to the peasant clothes. Something, a shadow, the vague illusion of an idea, insinuated itself at first and then fell in slow drops which accumulated, sped up by his breathing, and Álvaro wanted to see more. Audio, he needed the audio: he wanted to hear everything, understand everything. During the night they spent at the Seagull, the camera had recorded without stopping, till the tape ended. He left the room, called Fabiana, and again there was no response. He found the TV in the living room and considered putting the tape into the VCR, but he couldn't summon the nerve. Then he went into the master bedroom, where he found a smaller TV. He took it back to his own room, connected the camera, and watched.

They were making love. Alicia was mounting him, they turned, and then he mounted her, and they turned again. Now he stood, showing off the power of his virility for the camera. She teased him. They laughed. He rewound. Their laughter was repeated. Álvaro was surprised to hear his wife's voice. He remembered that he knew that voice by heart, that its timbre was unmistakable when the tone went from the most extravagant eroticism to the most naïve sensuality. He remembered his erection and he had another erection, and then his body remembered the wetness that had oozed from between Alicia's legs that night. He remembered more. He remembered a moan amid countless other moans, hoarse and trusting, so familiar. There was Alicia, affectionate after climax. He was falling asleep; she protested, come on, Álvaro, a little more, she kissed his ear, blew into his nose, Álvaro waved his hand to shoo the mosquito, she rearranged her curls, which fell upon his sleepy face, she licked his neck, she spoke to him: Álvaro, don't be mean, give me a little kiss, he snorted, she laughed again, tickled him with her hair, he rolled over, she sat in front of the camera, Álvaro saw her breasts recorded on tape and hated the clerk because Alicia couldn't sleep and he was sleeping and now Alicia had disappeared and he was starting to wake up and his tears fell as he watched himself sleeping. For two hours the camera had insisted that nothing could happen to them; it captured his snores and her tender, annoyed gesture; now she took out a cigarette and then everything happened as he and Casero had imagined it, she was about to go downstairs, and Álvaro's skin crawled, he saw her put on her grubby, sweaty T-shirt with ALICIA on the chest; now she put on her red pants, walking back and forth in the room; she entered the frame of the shot and exited again, but she reappeared, searching for her sandals when something happened and she turned her gaze toward the window. She walked over to the window, drew the curtain, raised the blinds, and looked. Álvaro rewound. Alicia was looking for her sandals; something was happening. Álvaro rewound again, turned up the volume, now you could hear a *pop*, like a cottony thud, again the tape ran backward, *pop*, another *pop*, and he began to understand, *pop*, and Alicia turned away, and the *pop* that was happening was a gunshot, dull, distant, extremely faint; far from Álvaro's range of hearing, the shot called out to Alicia, who went over to the window, raised the blinds, drew the curtain, and witnessed a scene that the camera could never record. She looked for a moment, then observed Álvaro, who was still placidly asleep, noticed his breathing, a fleeting snore; he turned over, and Alicia looked out the window again. There was a gesture, captured in three-quarter profile view, a gesture that might have been one of surprise, of fright, of rage. She turned away, put on her sandals and left the room. The tape went on for a while longer, and Álvaro continued watching himself in bed, so happy and grateful, asleep till the screen filled up with shiny, shrill black, white, and gray spots.

OFFERTORIUM

ОБЕРНУВШИСЬ

$\{IX\}$
DOMINE JESU

1) BREAKING A LOCK IS VERY SERIOUS BUSINESS

At precisely five o'clock he broke the lock and called Casero. The phone rang twice, and the lawyer answered.

"Did you find out anything?" Casero asked, without preliminaries.

"Alicia went downstairs in the early hours of the morning, at twelve fifty-three, to be precise."

"How do you know that?"

"It's recorded. My camera was working; it registers the date and the hour."

"I need to see that tape," the lawyer demanded.

"You can't."

"Whaddya mean, I can't? We can make a huge stink, go to the press. It's essential to study what it shows."

"You don't understand—it's a very personal tape, and I'm not showing it to anyone. Besides, it doesn't show much, but you can see that she heard something, a gunshot, I think. She looked out the window and went downstairs. Besides, the police have already seen it, but they didn't even touch it."

"They went into your room?"

"The clerk—I don't know his name—must have gone off delighted after looking at my sex life. He watched it on the viewfinder, and since the audio doesn't work well on that function, it didn't capture the shot. Look, maybe he didn't get as far as that scene. We came a while earlier."

"Mainieri. That guy's is such an asshole; it's better to stay out of his way. He's capable of killing you out of pure stupidity. I have two pieces of news. Your wife was at the hospital."

"Didn't you tell me she hadn't been there? Mother Aurora was surprised you believed that."

"And I was surprised that Mother Aurora thought I was so naïve. What I did was to verify their denial that she stopped by there. Álvaro, I wanted to spare you that moment because it's a delicate matter for you to ask those questions. But I have a nurse friend who gets very chatty in the sack. I spent most of an afternoon—a pretty hot afternoon—with her. She says that Alicia was brought in by three guys, around one AM. She didn't appear to be wounded, but if there was nothing wrong with her, why bring her in? She was there for an hour, and then they took her away; she doesn't know where. Three hours later the Chief came by, said he was doing rounds, asked if everything was in order, stayed for a couple of mates, and left."

"And what does that mean?"

"Chiefs of police don't make rounds, even in a shithole town like this."

"Who brought her in?"

"Romano and Mainieri, who else. I don't think you know the third one; his name is Tanco."

"I know him. He's the reason I'm here."

"You're out of your mind, son. People like that—you've gotta avoid them like the devil."

"How am I supposed to know who I'm talking to? The guy showed up out of nowhere and offered to help. In the middle of the desert I didn't have too many choices. My wife didn't like him at all, but we did what he told us. At least she's alive."

"At one AM she was. After that I don't know what might've happened."

"So what's the other piece of news?" Álvaro asked, trying to drive the doubt away.

"Mother Aurora probably told you."

"She said lots of things."

"That night there was a hunt."

"I don't know what you're talking about. She never mentioned anything like that," Álvaro lied.

"She probably doesn't know what happened; no one tells her anything."

"What kind of stories are these? What are you talking about? Okay, you're right, Mother Aurora told me that story, but I think she's not right in the head, what can I tell you, just look at her. People don't do things like that, Casero, don't be ridiculous," he insisted. That business of the disabled children and nighttime hunters still sounded like nonsense to him.

"Look, if you stop by my office, we can talk more openly."

"I think you're a little paranoid, Casero. Everybody here is kind of paranoid."

"In Las Casas it's a sign of mental health, and I'd rather see your face. Come right now; there's still time."

"Time for what?"

"Before it gets dark."

"I don't know... look, I need to think. What's the nurse's name?"

"I'm not gonna tell you."

"I can find out."

"You'll fuck yourself up, and you'll fuck up the nurse, too. Don't be so stubborn; come to my office. If it gets dark, you can stay over."

"What the hell happens at night? Do the vampires come out?"

"You're gonna die an idiot, boy. Don't come if you don't

want to. I still have to make a couple of calls."

"I'm on my way," Álvaro grumbled, and hung up.

2) A LIFT IN HIS SHOE

The law office was in the business district, two blocks from the orphanage, on the fifth floor of the only office building in town, between a kiosk and an electrical appliance store. The building was called Huemul I, and apparently had been the beginning of a lavish, but unfinished, growth period, which could be seen from the very entrance, in an advance state of decomposition due to humidity. A broken pipe, seemingly leaking water since the beginning of time, had peeled the paint off the walls, leaving black and green mold stains.

Álvaro crossed the threshold, saw the empty elevator cage, and stopped at the accordion door. He pressed the button, and when he let go, a harsh creak made him realize that the process could take some time. He rang again, and heard a metallic screech, a yawn, coming from up there. The elevator seemed to realize that someone was calling it, but before abandoning its long sleep, it likely needed to make a stop at the bathroom, followed by breakfast, and, finally, the decision to react. He released the button, and the metallic screech stopped again. He pushed a few more times, setting off a bitter, ill-tempered howl, some shaking, and, once again, silence.

He looked up: these were ancient floors, too high, and the staircase available to the public freed the building's owner of all responsibility for any accidents caused by using the elevator. He decided to climb the five flights of stairs, convincing himself all the while that he would never get there, cursing out the lawyer and humanity in general. By the time he arrived, his legs were aching and he was out of breath. Still panting, he walked down the dark hallway till he found the door to the law office:

DR. LAUREANO CASERO,
CRIMINAL, CIVIL, AND COMMERCIAL ATTORNEY-AT-LAW

The designation "International" was missing, but that made sense. The door, like the rest of the building, was in ruins. It was a wooden panel with frosted glass and several scratches, which formed a triangle in one corner where the glass had fallen out. Álvaro peeked through the hole and saw the lawyer sitting at his desk, his shirt sleeve rolled up and held in place by a rubber band on his left arm. His right hand held a syringe. Álvaro knocked.

"One moment, please," said Casero in a muffled voice. And then: "Okay, come in, come in."

Álvaro opened the door and entered. He walked directly over to the desk, as the lawyer finished giving himself the injection.

"What are you doing, Casero?"

"Don't get scared, it's insulin. I'm a diabetic."

"I didn't know you could inject insulin into a vein," Álvaro observed.

"I shoot it up my ass if necessary, and it's none of your fucking business what I do with my life," Casero replied sweetly, placing the vial on his desk.

"Just as long as you don't fuck up mine…"

"Try not to fuck up your own. From what I can see, you're doing a pretty good job."

"This is why you made me come?" asked Álvaro, twisting his neck in order to read the contents of the vial.

Casero pushed it toward him, saying:

"Read to your heart's content. I don't want you to go blind." Álvaro read a typewritten label stuck to the vial: it said "Insulin." Then, perturbed, he raised his head and looked the lawyer in the eye.

"What'd I come for, Casero?"

"You didn't know what you were talking about before. The hunt, I mean."

"The nun told me a ridiculous story about children and

the witch hunts they had two centuries ago. According to her, sick kids are born in this town. She said a lot of crazy stuff about the patients in her Home who disappeared and rich kids' entertainment. Frankly, man, this is the end of the millennium, and as far as I'm concerned, those stories make no sense."

"The meaning is in the story. Look," said the lawyer, showing him his short leg, the shoe with the lift, "it's hard to wiggle out of this. Here, the people who don't have deformities on the outside have them on the inside. Strange, isn't it? This town is a feudal fiefdom, Álvaro; it has an owner, and the owner's name is Dupree. You know two of them, but it's a whole family, a clan, really. Here we do whatever they want. Democracy was left behind, beyond the garbage dump. If this town seems forgotten, it's because that's what they've decided. And there's a kind of tradition. This place is full of deformed people, and they themselves don't try to get away. Look at the mayor: you've probably met his wife, too. But no matter: every so often the guys go out to fulfill their history by organizing a hunt. Mother Aurora must have told you about the demons; that's just nonsense, but they won't let it go, so then they go out and grab some kid from the Home. It's not hard. What could the Mother Superior do?"

"But she was recommended by the Vatican. She's not alone."

"Ah, but that doesn't matter; she can't do a fucking thing about it. And no one from the Vatican ever asks a thing about it. Go figure what's being cooked up in the world; we're so far away. It's a game; you've got to accept it that way. They grab some fairly agile kid—it can't be one that's bedridden; that wouldn't be sporting, you see—they set him loose in the nighttime and give him time to hide. Then they hunt him down. And if they don't find him because he found a good hiding place, most likely the wild dogs get him in the end." Casero paused; he appeared calm. "That's why no one goes out at night, get it? It's better to stay home and watch HBO; why would anyone want to get involved, if you can collect a few pesos, besides? I think that's what happened to your wife. She showed up in the middle of the shooting and they carried her off."

"And where is she now?" Álvaro asked, looking at the lawyer, who had closed his eyes. He was about to tap him on the arm when Casero opened his eyes and said:

"I'm trying to find out. I don't remember anything like this happening before; it can't be easy for them. It's one thing to blow away some messed up kid who nobody will ever ask about, but quite another to kidnap a woman who shows up by accident and whose husband is asking questions everywhere he goes. That's why I'm involved; look, I'm outside the action here; my... um, diabetes is eating me alive, and any minute now I'll go blind or have a heart attack. It's not worth it for them to get involved with me; it's like wasting gunpowder on birds, so once in a lifetime someone's got to mess them up by throwing a monkey wrench into the works."

"I've heard diabetics can't get it up."

"So?" Casero seemed to come fully awake.

"Well, earlier you were telling me about your chatty nurse friend."

"You don't trust me? What I do with a woman in bed is none of your concern, and if you think you can work things out yourself, then go to hell; I'm still planning to stick my nose wherever it fits. At this point I'm doing it as a sport," Casero politely explained. Now his eyes were shining and he seemed to be functioning smoothly.

"It's hard for me to believe you. You can't cover these things up forever; at some point..." Alvaro stopped and the lawyer finished the sentence:

"Something escapes from the equation and somebody comes to investigate. Is that what you were going to say?"

"Yes, but I don't think so. There must be a more logical explanation, political stuff, I don't know, maybe Alicia saw two guys fighting and... I don't know what to tell you."

"Listen, Álvaro, what we haven't figured out is where they took her. There aren't many places. One of them could be Dupree's estancia, but that would be unusual. They're not prepared to hold a kidnapped person; they don't do things like that."

"They must have killed her, then."

"I don't want to move so fast, son, not so fast. It's better to take it one step at a time. If there's no body, there's no murder. Why give up other possible paths? I've requested a writ of habeas corpus; it's not that the judge isn't trustworthy, but at least we'll complicate his life a little. And I've asked Mother Aurora to make an investigation at the Home. I want to know if a kid went missing that night. I don't think I'll find out a lot, but maybe we'll clear something up along those lines."

"Habeas corpus: you're funny. First you tell me that this is a fiefdom and people go out hunting down idiots, and now you come out with this crap. The only idiot hunted down here will be me."

"No, the only hunting victim that matters to you is your wife; if you want to see her as an idiot, that's your problem. But you're wrong; she reacted just like the rest of the world would react."

"I think you're naïve, Casero."

"Think whatever you want. They're bullshitting us with this garbage about demons, but meanwhile nobody has anything real to say about it. If I manage to spread the story beyond this place and get some big shot interested in it, I'll die happy."

"Try not to die today."

"I'll do my best," the lawyer promised with a smile.

3) BUT WHAT IF THE LAWYER WAS WRONG?

The police car was parked at the door of the pensión. Álvaro walked in, ready for a fight, ready to lose, and ready to be taken away. Ready for them to take him to wherever his wife happened to be at that moment, eager to put an end to all of it, wanting to see her, wanting to disappear himself. He managed to think about all that when the door to the room swung open and he found Ayala and Mainieri watching the video.

"What are you doing?" he asked, articulating the question with the impression that he was one more victim about to be hunted down. His back tensed, his vertebrae ached, his breathing became labored, the veins in his neck bulged, and he had an urge to run away.

"Nice little filly you've got there, kid. Turn off the tape, Mainieri." Ayala stood and gave him a shove while Mainieri fiddled with the camera.

"Listen, kid, it'd be better if you stay in your own lane, you hear me? This ain't no joke, so listen up: we're working folks here. We do things the right way, and no city boy is gonna come here to investigate. We're a family, and families don't air their dirty laundry; they take care of things behind closed doors. Is that clear? You're in my town, and you're getting to be really annoying. Stay cool and stop screwing around; leave the Mongos alone, don't talk to that crazy bitch at the Home, dump the fucking lawyer—can't you see you're getting into trouble? And if you go on like this, things are gonna get real ugly for you. You've been warned, buddy. Here in Las Casas we don't beat around the bush."

"So I'm beginning to discover," Álvaro stammered, thinking of his video with the naked Alicia in the room.

"What are you discovering? Listen to me and listen good: If you pay attention to decent people, your luck will turn for the better. Right now you're floating with your head in the clouds. You're an outsider, and you don't get how things work around here, so get it straight right now: Your filly is at the morgue," Ayala informed him and left the room.

Álvaro was stunned. He assumed it was a joke, spun around, looked at the camera, and left to make a phone call.

"Casero, it's Álvaro. Ayala was at the pensión. He says Alicia is at the morgue." He was trembling.

"I'm on my way over there."

"But it's late now. It's almost dark."

"Don't be an idiot. Go to the morgue. It's two blocks away."

"The eviscerator's gone home."

"I know where he lives. I'll drag him by the ear."

They met at the door. Casero was standing next to the bald guy; without his work clothes he looked less sinister. They went inside, walked to the back room, and opened the refrigerator. Without saying a word, the eviscerator put on his synthetic apron and purple gloves, recovered his stony attitude, and pulled out the same bag as before.

"I told you to wait. It's got to be this one—who else could it be?" he remarked, struggling with the bag of remains.

"Shut your trap, Saverio. Let's see if you get it right for once in your life."

Álvaro took short little steps; he was still trembling. He watched the eviscerator fiddle with the bag, sweat dripping down his back, his cheeks reddening. He watched the bag come out of the refrigerator and land propped up on the floor. Saverio straightened it up and started to open the zipper. He gave it a yank, the bag fell, and Álvaro averted his eyes.

"What do you see?" he asked, staring at the ceiling.

"It's a woman," said Casero.

"The counselor's a real genius," said Saverio. "The woman is young—you already know that. Listen, *don*, why don't you take a look yourself and save me the trouble?"

Álvaro turned to the woman who sat in front of him. Her fallen head concealed her face.

"Raise her head, please," he asked.

Saverio pulled her head up by the hair.

"Slower, please, wait—what's that on her face?"

"Wounds, dog bites—I told you that, already. Do you recognize anything?"

"No, I don't know. You can't tell from the clothing—it's very dirty. What color are the pants?"

"They look brown; they could be red."

"Red? Is that possible?"

"Saverio, why don't you check the hem of her pants; that'll be in better condition."

"Because I'll have to take her out altogether and I want to see if the gentleman can make up his mind."

"The T-shirt is in bad shape, too. Is that a T-shirt?"

"It could be a sweatshirt, a T-shirt, how should I know?"

Álvaro looked at the woman's hands, but they were destroyed. You could see the bite marks; some fingers were missing. He asked to see her naked. Saverio snorted, took her out of the bag, and laid her on the floor.

"You'll have to excuse me for not putting her on a table, but they're all occupied," Saverio grumbled.

"It's okay. Would you mind stepping outside for a moment?"

"No, man. Take your time."

They left the room. Álvaro kneeled next to the body, trying not to heave. He removed the shreds of clothing she still had on, looked at the hem of her pants, but couldn't tell the color; the T-shirt was a shapeless patch of destroyed cloth. The body didn't reveal much: a woman, possibly young, pale, sticky, with dead blood pooled at the point of contact; the face inaccessible, the hair too dirty and caked with mud to permit any recognition. Nothing, not a familiar ring, her sandals, or even the slight scar on her devastated left cheek.

He gradually calmed down, observing with colder eyes. He looked for details, reminders, a wrinkle, the fold of her neck, a tiny birthmark, but nothing suggested that the woman might be Alicia. He stood up and called.

"How did they identify her? I can't find anything."

"It must have been by process of elimination," Saverio ventured.

"I have a different idea: they want this body taken away. With a little good will, it could just as easily be the First Lady,"

Casero remarked.

"That's not my wife," Álvaro decided, not knowing if that made him feel any better.

"Then you need to go home. It's not a good time for running around."

Álvaro picked up his pace as he walked back to the pensión. He looked at the sky. Night was swiftly falling, enveloping him. He had the sensation of being in some cheesy version of Dracula and felt abandoned. He still thought of Casero as an unreliable specimen; it would have been better to have Dr. Van Helsing as a friend. It wasn't insulin he'd been injecting, that much seemed pretty clear, and no matter what the label on the vial said, insulin was never injected into a vein. Mainieri's comment had reaffirmed that. He didn't know what he was doing. He'd let himself be carried along by the opinion of a guy who didn't deserve anyone's respect and who told him outrageous tales, who bought the story of the abandoned children and nighttime hunting expeditions—who could believe that nonsense? He walked along, and his head worked without consulting him. Now he realized that, despite his lack of confidence in the police, he was giving credence to their opinions. And that bothered him, too. They were as dishonest as Casero. He felt like a coward. He would have liked to believe in the official version, accept that unrecognizable body, take it home, and escape from his agony. If that corpse could be the First Lady, it could just as easily be Alicia.

{X}
HOSTIAS

1. RANTS AND GLIMMERS

Fabiana was waiting for him at the pensión; her expression was what he had expected. Álvaro glanced around, looking for El Tolo, but he was nowhere nearby.

"You're going to have to leave," Fabiana informed him. The broken lock was in her hand.

"You're right—I'll go first thing tomorrow morning. I'll pay you whatever you say. None of this is your fault."

"You don't understand—you're leaving right now," Fabiana said. Her face was marble.

"I can't now; your husband told me not to go out at night."

"That's not my problem. I don't want the police in my house. Go get your stuff and leave right away."

"What about my car?"

"Go to the auto shop. El Tolo usually sleeps there; ask him for it."

Álvaro grabbed his things and ran over to the shop. The car was parked by the door with the keys in the ignition. The metal blinds were closed. He knocked, and El Tolo's voice answered immediately, not even bothering to ask who it was.

"Get into your car and stay there. Don't leave, and don't let them see you. The car's not ready, so don't turn the motor over because it won't work; the only thing you'll accomplish is letting them hear you."

"What the fuck is going on? Why are you doing this to me?"

"It's not about you, it's about us. Get down and everything'll be all right."

"Who's not gonna see me? Why don't you open the door?" Álvaro banged on the metal blinds, shouting; the noise echoed all along the block.

"Stop making such a racket; they'll hear you," replied El Tolo from behind the blinds. A window high above them opened, someone cursed, demanding silence, and the window closed again.

Álvaro turned around, got into the car and locked the door from inside. He tried to calm down, looked ahead and behind, lit a cigarette, and turned on the radio. Frankie Laine was singing "Sixteen Tons," and nothing moved; no people could be heard, no one went by. He lowered the volume and took a drag. The air grew thin and his eyes teared. He couldn't breathe, so he lowered the window a little. A gust of cold air blew in and his eyes cleared. He bundled up in his leather jacket and found a comfortable position on the seat; the yellow avenue kept blinking. The wind dragged a few leaves along, and when Frankie Laine stopped singing, the swings began to creak.

"Good evening, friends in Los Huemules," said the radio, "this is LUK76 FM , Las Casas, broadcasting for all the insomniacs, all those lonely folks out there, and for those working till dawn, our brothers on the graveyard shift, the pharmacists, doctors, police officers. Well, I could include myself on that list, in all modesty... Here we are at our usual number, call us, we're ready to hear your request; as you know, my name is Charlie the Chimp, at least that's what they call me. You've just heard Frankie Laine with 'Sixteen Tons,' a classic from the fifties, those beloved years, those wonderful times that will come back one day, of course they will; hand in hand we'll make it happen. You're listening to LUK76, Las Casas, your friendly radio station. Let's see, what's happening in Los Huemules... As all of you know, Mayor Dupree is determined to launch us into the nation and into the world, because it's time for our town to emerge from obscurity and for the world to know we're here, working and striving, all of us hand in hand, to improve our children's education, to provide our beloved regional hospital with medications, bandages, surgical equipment, and to give our security forces all the necessary infrastructure for this town to continue to be the most peaceful in the country: these are our mayoral office's objectives. And let it be known, neighbors in Los Huemules, that it goes beyond that fact that here in our town, your daughter can go out alone at night and nothing will happen to her because this is the safest of towns, a town of families. People here get educated and get healed; that's our task, and the mayor is the faithful representative of our most heartfelt sentiments. Today, for example, we opened our second elementary school, which includes two computers, twenty new desks, and all the necessary supplies for our children to progress in their learning, without setbacks or wavering. And also, without setbacks or hesitation, tomorrow the mayor will present a new CT machine to the children's wing at the hospital, because all our effort is for their sake. Finally, this weekend Chief of Police Ayala will receive two police cars, complete with the latest equipment needed for improved and more efficient vigilance, so that our children can go out in the streets safely and peacefully. It'll be a real festival, and the municipal band will be on hand to entertain us. It'll be worth your while to come down to the police station—at the end of the ceremony there will be wine and empanadas. Well, my friends, that was today's news, and now for our musical interlude and some messages: Manuel the baker—we all know him, of course—announces that his delicious Easter cakes will be available tomorrow, so get ready to enjoy them, because that wonderful holiday of meditation and remembrance of Our Lord Jesus Christ will soon be here. Manuel requests a tune by Frankie Laine, 'Sixteen Tons.' With pleasure, Manuel. Okay, this one's for Manuel, hoping that he'll remember us with one of his delicious Easter cakes, here we go with Manuel's request. I'm your host, Charlie the Chimp, and this is LUK76."

The voice was calming and soothing, and yet Álvaro wondered if they hadn't just played that same song. He couldn't be sure, but it seemed strange to him. He looked down the street, where the avenue ran, yellow and silent. The barely audible volume didn't hide the city's powerful stillness. Álvaro waited, closed his eyes, and slept, or at least that was what he thought, and he never asked himself that question again because suddenly his eyes were wide open, and he was still sitting in his car. Charlie the Chimp was reading other messages, or maybe it was the same one, and Frankie Laine was still crooning gently and soothingly when Álvaro heard a noise like the clashing of smooth hooves, a lightness approaching along the avenue. He unfolded his body, opened the door, walked until the yellow light enveloped him, and then, right before him, he saw a huemul. The animal was grazing beside a tree; it trotted a little, stopped, raised its head, and Álvaro could tell by its antlers that it was young. He couldn't believe his eyes. The huemul turned toward him, opened its snout, breathed on Álvaro, nodded its head and resumed grazing. Nothing else happened: the huemul's smooth hooves resounded on the asphalt, and it seemed like Frankie Laine, somewhere off in the distance, might have been crooning to that apparition. Then, like a burst of fear erupting, there was a boom, and Álvaro woke. A desperate face pressed against the window on his side. He couldn't escape his dream, or perhaps his dream had taken the form of a nightmare. The face was a frightened mask of horror and desperation, a little boy who was begging for help. Álvaro shook his head from side to side, and the disabled child, who seemed to understand that those were the inviolable rules of the game, ran away, yelping with fear, and disappeared into the darkness. Álvaro hunkered down, unwilling to see anymore. Another shot rang out, followed by urgent voices, energetic footsteps of men who might have been wearing boots. A dog barked, then a few more; the barking was coming toward Álvaro; then a pack of dogs stopped next to the car door. The beasts sniffed, they reared on their hind feet, and Álvaro saw the mastiffs' paws and snouts sliding along the window and the windshield; they climbed on the hood and the roof, growling quietly, holding back the rage of the hunt; their paws and snouts searched, and they panted around and above Álvaro, who pressed against the seatback and sank his head between his shoulders, possibly observed by those furious eyes. He watched the maws and fangs clash against the glass and metal, making a tense music amid foaming mouths and horrid tongues. As if broadcasting from another planet, Charlie congratulated someone on their daughter's fifteenth birthday. The dogs howled, called out, abandoned the trail, making way for the boots and shouts, rumbling along, loading their weapons, poking around with their flashlights; at last the pack gave up on the car and moved away, following the exact path of their prey; and behind them ran the men, several, many, possibly twenty men calling and announcing the direction taken by the dogs; all of them vanished into the shadows. Álvaro heard the echoes growing distant as Frankie Laine—again!—began to sing "Sixteen Tons," now requested by someone whose name he didn't catch, and he wondered, confused, if they played only one tune at that radio station. As in his dream of the huemul, or perhaps his wakefulness, he opened the door, gripping his camera, and walked in the same direction as the dogs and the men. He went, and though he knew he shouldn't go, he also knew that he would find the direction he was looking for. He turned the corner, studied the darkness, and turned on the camera, noticing the pattern of movements and howls. They were hunting. Intense flashlight beams pierced the night in the black depths of the avenue; they were shooting right and left, lighting up trees and shrubs, forward and backward. They seemed confused; the prey moved without cunning, retracing its steps and following the same paths again and again. Only the dogs understood the unexpected trail that snaked around without finding a way out. A shot exploded, and there was the cry of a wounded animal. Someone swore at someone else over the life of his bullet-ridden dog, and the reply was a worse insult, followed by laughter and expletives. Álvaro walked over to the edge of the shadow; he sensed the scattered presence of the men. The camera captured dark figures and branches trampled by boots. A snort passed by along the opposite path, ignoring him, and returned a moment later; a flashlight sank to the ground, illuminating a bulk that was still breathing. The bulk looked white, and Álvaro thought he saw a wounded mastiff. And his camera recorded, recorded, never stopping; it registered whatever was there, footsteps running, sparks, a cry, a gunshot, two, it was possible that it even recorded a tumult of shouting puppets, but Álvaro kept documenting. Farther along, the hunting expedition continued, relentless. Now other lights, followed by hoarse voices, were running, seemingly in circles. Álvaro hid in a garden; the windows and doors of the house would remain closed till the inevitable dawn, and he knew this too, hidden behind a shrub. He knew that that shrub was his life, and also as far as he would go on that night when animals never slept and hunters persisted till at last—maybe an hour later, after a furious hail of bullets—they came upon their trophy, now mortally wounded. There was the sound of the coup de grâce, then howls and hurrahs of victory, bottles uncorked and the final march toward the desert, bearing the prey's body in the trunk of a big black car. They would leave it there, Álvaro understood, because that was where the wild dogs were, and they did the dirty work; they finished the task cleanly.

Álvaro turned off the camera. He didn't know when he fell asleep.

2) ENCOUNTER AT THE AUTO SHOP

Álvaro was awakened by a shotgun. Clutching his camera, asleep, and still terrified, curled up in a ball behind the shrub in the garden of the house with closed windows, he took a while to open his eyes and confront at last, the hostile gaze of two barrels interested in his forehead with their hammers anxious to fire.

The doors to the house were open now, he noticed. From the window a boy was watching him, guided away a moment later by his mother's hand. Facing the shotgun, Álvaro offered explanations; he managed to invent a blackout—a nervous condition, he argued, epilepsy, he said, and also loss of consciousness. He swore to the shotgun that he had no idea how he arrived at the place; he apologized a million times and kept begging for forgiveness till the barrels pointed toward the sky and the weapon asked if he felt all right, but the tone of the question was still one of unyielding distance. Yes, he replied, yes sir, he felt better, he stammered and struggled to stand; the barrels were lowered a little, but not enough. Álvaro extended his arms, palms down, never ceasing to explain that, no doubt about it, what he was going to do right now was to see a doctor, at the same time loyally offering his I.D. documents so that the owner of the house would stop distrusting him, a situation that would still take much too long to occur, and since it wasn't a matter of wasting their lives on such trivial business, Álvaro remained alert and the man's voice never stopped sounding hard and hostile as he finally pointed out the familiar path to the door; the rifle itself marked the way, appropriately enough; that man clutching his camera must be the famous Martian, recently arrived from the desert skies, an unclassifiable stranger, an annoying, disgusting pest, full of questions, someone who should never be trusted, awake or asleep.

Álvaro followed the path indicated by the weapon. He thanked the feudal lord of the manor for his great generosity after having his house invaded by such a detestable person, and he apologized again, with an affected gesture, reminiscent of a fawning peasant from some Kurosawa film, and feeling his misery touch an as-yet-unfamiliar bottom.

As he left he realized that he had peed his pants, and in a wretched way he felt relieved because he hadn't exactly lied: that's what happens to all epileptics.

He went to find his car, which was still at the shop. El Tolo's greasy legs still poked out from underneath; by this time they seemed like part of the car. He opened the door, took out the bag, and El Tolo asked who was there.

"It's me," Álvaro replied, and disappeared into the bathroom. He washed up, changed his pants, came out, sat on the only bench and waited for El Tolo to come to a full standing position. He had briefly considered grabbing the mechanic by his lapels and punching the shit out of him till he talked and apologized, but he stopped when he saw the tool, an impressively large adjustable wrench that El Tolo held in his right hand. But his fury was still alive.

"You son-of-a-bitch, you left me outside all night," he said through clenched teeth, looking at the tool.

"I couldn't do anything, please understand," the mechanic answered with an aggrieved expression, as he laid the wrench on the ground.

"What am I supposed to understand? They kill people in this town, and everybody closes their doors. I'm supposed to understand that all of you are fucked up, you're a bunch of sons-of-bitches, fucking bastards; I could've taken a bullet and no one would've done a thing. Who's behind all this? Who pulled the trigger last night? Why don't the police throw them all in jail?"

"Lower your voice." El Tolo made a gesture: the police car was passing by, driven by Mainieri, who turned his head toward Álvaro and continued on his way. El Tolo took out a sign that read CLOSED DUE TO ILLNESS and lowered the metal blinds. "You still don't get it at all," he finally whispered.

"What didn't I understand?" Álvaro said. "Last night they killed a kid; smashed his head like a coconut. Do you understand *that*? He had a mental disability, a poor kid without a fully functioning brain who couldn't even defend himself; they hunted him down with guns and dogs, and then they finished him off. The took him away in a black car and threw him out into the desert. There's nothing to understand. Everyone in this town is crazy; at night they kill people and the next day off they go to work. What's going on here? Do you know where my wife is?" Álvaro softened his voice, but not his tone. "Nobody gives a shit; the only one who threw me a line is Casero, who's strung out all the time."

"Nobody's gonna help you," El Tolo said in an expressionless voice. "The best thing you can do is get the fuck out of here right now. Your car's ready."

"You're a real shit," Álvaro whispered. "I'm not going anywhere. First I want to know where my wife is."

"Look," El Tolo sighed, "this is nothing new, and it's not about rich kids or absent-minded cops. Around here everybody does their own job. I know it's not clear, but that's the way it's always been. They call the orphanage The Sanctuary."

"And what does Mother Aurora have to say about it?"

"She can't do anything. I don't know if she cares that much, honestly; if she became difficult, if she used her contacts at the Vatican—if they really exist and aren't just stories she's made up—and if by some chance they answered her from back there, just imagine what the answer would be. What do you think? A Church investigation into a little town lost in the middle of the desert? You really believe that one state is going to confront another over a couple of fucked-up kids? The first thing they'd do would be to take her out of commission, a transfer to 'protect' her, and you can put that word in quotes. Where could she go? All she has is the Home; the orphans are her life, they're the kids she never had."

El Tolo paused, seeming to measure what was about to follow.

"Sometimes a person shuts his eyes over one lost kid, just so they won't lose all of them. All she can do is be outraged."

"What about the orphanage's registry? Something would certainly come out of those."

"There are no registries; they just list the untouchables. Dupree's son, for example."

"And how do you know?"

"I used to hunt," replied El Tolo, staring at his wrench on

the ground.

Álvaro took a step backward.

"Come here." El Tolo walked toward a rear patio. Álvaro recognized the black car parked beneath the grapevine.

"Why are you showing me this?"

"They keep it here. They still trust me, I guess. Fact is, they're a pack of liars. Before, they used to say it was a crusade, a holy mission. Father Dupree had fire in his words; he taught us that there was a curse, that we needed to work in order to save the town. The deformed children were the curse, the half-breeds, people born of forbidden unions. Fathers who've slept with their daughters, that's what you see most. There are also lots of cases of brothers and sisters doing it; there were cases where a mother got pregnant by her own son; sometimes you couldn't even figure out which son it was. I don't know—maybe it's something that comes from the Indians; people from the town have mixed a lot with them. Genetic defects, maybe. Those things were always very common in town, so it was necessary to make strict rules, to get rid of that filth and clean the blood. If you think about it, their intentions weren't bad; it was pretty civilizing. Them, the defectives that were born, they were the devil incarnate, see? Like at the beginning of history, you had to fight against Evil. Evil was disguised as a poor devil, but it was a devil, after all. That might sound old-fashioned to you; sure, it really seems like a load of crap, but people in this town are very passive. Or maybe they only care about what suits them. I don't know if anybody really believed it; I suppose there were people who took it seriously. Look, me too, I wanted to believe I was doing what had to be done. And besides, the Dupree family is too powerful, and it doesn't seem sensible to doubt the boss's words. There was this wild idea: they insisted that the Devil was organizing his legions, but it wasn't official, you know? It was an open secret, those poor kids were the Devil's armies, and they frightened people with the warning that the Antichrist was about to be born."

He stopped for a moment. "Yeah, it's sad to think about it.

So the orphanage turned into a detention center for the aborted creatures from hell, that's what they called them, like the first Dupree. It was a holding pen—they kept them till they were ready. I believed in that; I believed that the Church supported us, when in fact what they did was to look the other way. When I understood what was happening, I asked them to release me. Health problems, I claimed. I was a sailor and I was afraid of losing my job, so they looked at me with mistrust; they asked questions that would confuse the sharpest guy, but look, I suppose they understood that I had been a collaborator and I would never think of revealing anything, because, in any case, nobody would believe me. I'm not a trustworthy sort of guy, you understand. I was there, I squeezed the trigger, and then I left the kids in the desert. You know how many times I drove that car? I thought I was a hero, but the truth is, I'm a murderer and I'll never go to prison. They thanked me for my service, they gave me a medal, and they let me go. Since then I've devoted myself to sailing, and when I'm home, I fix engines."

"And why do they hunt them down now?"

"That business was a war, they told us, but they never declared peace. I really don't know who they were going to sign the treaty with, and besides, I imagine they got into the habit. Like tigers—they tried human blood and they got a taste for it. If you want to know the truth, I still believe in all that. It's the only thing I've ever done in my life, the only really important thing."

The two men fell silent. Álvaro lit a cigarette, looked at a fallen piston rod, the grease stains all around it, the blinds that filtered the light from below. He swallowed hard and held back his tears.

"Do you know anything about my wife?" he asked, and there was a rock stuck in his throat.

"No."

Álvaro walked toward his car. He turned the motor over; it started.

"How much do I owe you?"

"Nothing."

Álvaro looked at him, then pulled a random bill from his wallet, rolled it up into a ball, and threw it onto the greasy floor, near the piston rod. Then he got into the car and took off.

3) THE BOYS IN THE BAR

Álvaro drove away from the auto repair shop; in his rear view mirror he saw the inverted image of El Tolo standing by the door, watching him go. He turned the corner and crossed the avenue. When he passed in front of the bar, the customers stared at him from their tables. He thought that someone there might be able to give him... something, he didn't know exactly what to expect, a little encouragement, small-town solidarity... He was hungry; he hadn't eaten since the day before. He couldn't even remember when. He entered the bar, and the silence was the same as the stares, previous and current. Now they stopped everything again to watch him walk in: the truco game and the gin stopped; the beans froze in their trajectory from one pile to another; some glasses halted in their march toward the customers' lips, while others returned, intact or already consumed, to the coaster. The waiter wiped off an empty table, and the cleanup slowed momentarily; a hoarse voice lowered in volume, becoming a murmur; a dairyman's laughter was interrupted; a joke hung in the air without a punchline: everyone was looking, except Romano, who kept his eyes on some fixed point in his glass of gin.

Álvaro ordered something quick along with a soda. They brought him two empanadas and a Coke, and the customers elbowed one another, smiled, whispered, laughed softly, ordered wine. Álvaro asked for the bill; they called out the amount from behind the counter; he placed the money on the table and left.

Romano never raised his eyes from his glass.

4) THE MAYOR FLOATED IN A LAKE OF ASHES

Álvaro stopped the car in front of the large entrance door, and someone from Security approached him, but he didn't need to explain anything. The guard made a phone call and a moment later the door was opened. It was a cloudy day, and there was no one in the swimming pool, but the discreet surveillance hadn't moved. The tires crunched over the gravel path up to the white staircases. The maid in her uniform and headdress guided him along the corridors lined with huemul heads and unfamiliar paintings with authentic signatures, although this time she turned down some unexplored pathway and showed him into a different room, in the middle of which was a bathtub the size of a medium swimming pool. It seemed to Álvaro that it was made of gold, though it might have been just a good quality gold plating. Behind the headrest of the tub was a bar, and in front of it a TV screen like the one he had seen on his previous visit. It must have been a different one, he thought; he could hardly believe the fat man had moved that TV set just to take a bath. A huge, white, hairless bulk—he found himself thinking of Gregory Peck, lame and hallucinating, prepared to fight Moby-Dick to the death—floated amid explosions of suds. Dupree's breasts shook with the death throes of that great belly, crowned with the froth of bath salts, undoubtedly French, Álvaro guessed, and a small lake balanced grudgingly on the peak where that peaceful, extensive navel dwelt. At the side of that great white cetacean, a cigar burned, dangling from the mouth of a surprisingly stable, yellow rubber duck; the concavity in the duck's back allowed it to double as an ashtray, and, in a vague way, a visual echo of the navel. The fat man, lazy and placid, his mouth coated with bits of food at the corners, chewed as he watched his gigantic TV and smiled absently. When he noticed Álvaro standing off to one side, he was startled, but he regained his composure and turned off the sound: a soccer game was on, and the commentator's voice was cut off in the middle of a goal that threatened to become eternal.

"What do you want now?" He reached out his arm and grabbed the long, fat cigar. The little rubber duck trembled but remained heroically upright.

"To find out if you've heard anything."

"Did you go to the places I told you about?"

"Some of them."

"Where?"

"You know where I was, Dupree. I went to the police station to ask, but their Chief doesn't seem to be interested or intelligent enough: he told me that my wife's body was at the morgue. I went there, but I didn't recognize her. Explain to me how he could have recognized her. Ayala is an arrogant jerk; he tried to hand me any corpse with a smashed face for me to take home, which means he's also an idiot, if you want my opinion. Are those the honest people who are going to defend the fatherland?"

"You'd better watch that insolent tongue of yours," Dupree advised, flicking a thick fragment of ashes onto the duck, which began to rock from side to side. "If Chief Ayala told you that the body was your wife's, I have no right to doubt his good intentions, but he might have been mistaken."

"I don't know how the regulations work around here, but in the rest of the world, bodies are identified by relatives or close friends, never the police. And I have Alicia's documents in my possession, in case there's any doubt," Álvaro replied. Dupree stubbed out the cigar on the back of the rubber duck, which started listing to one side. The ashes spilled over into the bath water, darkening the foam, and the cigar floated nearby, carried along by dark, delicate, internal currents. The mayor moved, graceful and distinguished, generating restrained waves, till, at last, he sat at the bottom of his bathtub. Álvaro watched the duck's butt floating inexorably upward and felt like he was about to drown.

"In any case, you should have gone to him again and asked him about it."

"After he went into my own room and went through my stuff? After he watched my private videos without my permission? If there was a search warrant, he didn't show it. Do you think he had one? I doubt it, even though I think it doesn't matter. And not only did he give me a shove, he threatened me. Should I report him for brutalizing and threatening me at his police station? What do you recommend, Dupree? What would you do with somebody who invades your privacy?" asked Álvaro, desperately wishing that the duck would poke its head out of the water.

"Young and indiscreet visitor to my town, you are a feisty city intellectual, with very progressive ideas and a shady police record: don't do the very thing you're criticizing; don't invade my privacy, I beg of you," replied Dupree very deliberately and appearing to spell out each word as he looked at Álvaro from the immensity of his bathtub, amid ashy bubbles of foam and waves that came and went, generated by the fat man's movements. The duck appeared to have definitively drowned.

"I suppose that privacy is a rare commodity around here, and hard to get."

"You suppose right. You invaded my house, let's say by mistake, and as everybody knows, in his own house a man is king, though if you want to know the truth, around here I decide more than a simple… um, homegrown king, let's put it that way. It's my responsibility as leader; you'll understand that I can't let myself be swayed by mere personal desires; I need to soar like an eagle and have a clear view of the landscape, which is the right way of doing politics. It's possible that Ayala doesn't like you because of some question of character, or a regional bias, if you will, but I don't think it's an insurmountable problem. We're here for more important purposes, my young friend, and maybe you should think things over more carefully before relying on people you didn't even know yesterday. That nun, to give you an example, isn't well in the only part of her body she has, her head, and, to be honest, I doubt she'll stay on in such a responsible position, though, of course, that's not up to me to decide. And that lawyer? Well, young man, it doesn't take too much mental clarity to figure out that he's someone who's lost his way. He keeps bad company, that one, but of course you're a free, responsible man and you can talk to anyone you please. In any case, I'm the only one who can help you, I'm telling you, and I'm not in the habit of talking to strangers. Your case worries me; my town's reputation is at stake, and that's worth a lot in Las Casas. And you'll agree that the most important thing for you is still your wife's fate. Be calm, young man, and arm yourself with patience. Don't stress over little conflicts that won't change the heart of the matter. In all small towns, people tend to be suspicious, and we're not too polished here. Sometimes we go overboard and we seem worse than we really are, but this is a town of working people, good people, a little crazy, like I said, but loyal and devout. Loyalty is one of my neighbors' virtues. Remember that and go back to your pensión."

"I can't, the owner threw me out. The Police Chief's visit was too much for her, and believe me, I understand. I have nowhere to go."

"Well, don't despair; you'll find somewhere soon. There are simple, generous people here who can rent you their back room for hardly any money. For a few cents. Or for nothing. This is a Christian town, and solidarity is a Christian virtue. You're Catholic, aren't you?"

"No."

5) THE FALLEN ANGEL

They watched the tape. The lawyer's VCR was old, and the tracking was shot: the images looked jumbled; there were too many dark shapes, flashes accompanying the gunshots, voices that didn't mean anything to Álvaro and that Casero recognized without hesitation: Mainieri, a few times, sounding out of control; Ayala, of course, cursing out his clerk for shooting the mastiff.

"Nero," said the lawyer.

"Who?" Álvaro asked.

"Nero, the mastiff," Casero explained, just as Romano's voice was inevitably heard, demonstrating command in his tone; more shapes came along running and passing by, and there was howling; the branches of the shrub where Álvaro had taken shelter covered up the scene; a familiar, furious barrage of gunshots was heard; there were celebrations, victory cries, the black car's doors were flung open; they threw a dark shape into the trunk; now it passed in front of the camera; there was Ayala's round, distant, and barely recognizable face at the wheel; the car turned right; the license plate was visible, though not the numbers; hoots of laughter exploded, along with a few shots into the air: a traditional sound of celebration.

Casero removed the cassette from the machine and poured himself a whiskey, then lit a cigarette and sat down. He smoked, drank, and smoked again. They were silent.

"This is very strong stuff, but I think it's poor evidence. Can the image be sharpened?" Casero asked after a while.

"The audio's not bad and there are ways of sharpening the image if you do it right; I know about all that stuff. An edit island and a powerful computer would help me, and if they had a digitizing video card..." Álvaro stopped short. "Do you think we could get something like that around here?"

"Of course." Casero smiled. "The general store has everything. Consider it done, nothing simpler than finding cutting-edge technology in the middle of the desert. What color computer do you want?"

"Yesterday Mother Aurora told me about somebody who surfs the internet and then goes around kicking the feeble-minded."

"Ah, yes, that's... it's Romano's son. For sure he's on the tape. Do you want to ask him for help? I can give you his phone number." The lawyer's smile grew radiant.

"Give me solutions, Casero. I don't know this place," Álvaro pleaded.

"There's that kid, Charlie the Chimp—he's not exactly trustworthy, but he's selling a good computer, I think. We'll have to see if he'll agree to help."

"The one on the radio? How am I supposed to hand this over to that ass-kisser?"

"Everyone here's an ass-kisser, my boy. Except me—I'm the only official renegade, though it wasn't always like that. They spared my life, till now, at least. I'm gonna tell you something, to wise you up a little. Maybe it'll help you find your way around: In the old days, I did some big business with the Duprees, lots of times with phony papers." Casero downed a swig and continued talking: "Like the ones dealing with the priest's kid, for example. Those weren't the only dealings I had, of course, but that was quite a long time ago and it lasted till I fell out of favor. You've already realized that it wasn't insulin I was injecting the other day, right? You're not as dumb as you look. You'll understand that it's not easy for me to whitewash these things in front of somebody I hardly know; it would be easier to fix the glass panel on the door. It's been so many years of broken glass, working in plain view of the first guy to poke his head in, that I hardly notice it anymore. This apathy is only partly due to the morphine, which is sweet and a good companion; in fact, it's really something classic. When it comes, it stays, and every day it demands a little more. It's an insatiable wife who's also sort of a liar. You try it and you're in paradise, but only at first. In the end you're thankful if your whole body doesn't hurt, down to the hairs in your ass. And let's not even talk about high responsibility jobs, or low responsibility, for that matter. I was as high up as a person can go, and it all went to shit: now that's what I call a fall, Álvaro, and I suppose that's what made me untrustworthy in their eyes. Only that. Yeah, I'm a real nasty bastard but I'm not a traitor. In the end they got fed up and threw me out the window. It's a miracle they didn't throw me out in the desert. Let's say I'm a fallen angel, and Charlie, who also does his business with the owners of paradise, is my successor. He has that radio show and broadcasts official propaganda, but that's for fools. It's a tough thing to figure out: Why do some people become trustworthy without having too much to show for it? It could be because he never asks questions, but on the other hand, he always gives the right answers, something I stopped doing when the morphine got too expensive for me. Whatever the reason, there was Charlie, who always was a rat and suddenly became worthy of credit in their eyes, and then, logically, they bought him. And Mayor Dupree is a good paymaster; he really coughs up the necessary pesos. Besides, Charlie's business is broader; he sells *everything*, you know? And when I say everything, I mean everything, young girls for the heirs' parties, and little boys, too, who are a highly desirable commodity in Los Huemules and command such good prices, and if they want coke, Charlie brings them top-of-the-line stuff, uncut; of course it's super expensive, but there's no shortage of money for important occasions. And it's not that the guy's just a partier, don't believe it—he does a little arms trafficking too, if it's necessary, but he keeps a low profile, for sure, on the town level, you know: an Uzi here, some nice little pistol for Romano, a couple of grenades for the guy over there, crap for all the idiotic hangers-on who follow the fat guy around, just to keep them happy. Stick a weapon in their belts and—bingo!—you've got your loyal followers, everything nice and easy, you know, because Charlie, ah, Charlie doesn't get involved with heavy players, he's just a go-between, which confirms his status as a trustworthy guy. If the client pays, he gets him anything he wants. Ask him to show you the warehouse; for sure you'll find something useful there: computers, VCRs—he's got whatever you ask him for. These days he gets me morphine, which never was his specialty, and he charges me a fortune for every vial because he's the middleman's middleman, and that drives the prices up. Besides, he sells it to me at a discount, but that could be considered a favor to my health. I had a lot of money in those days; this building, for example, and a farm in Arizmendi. I raised breeding pigs; I even had a prize-winning stud and everything; the certificate should be around here somewhere. And I had reserves in the bank, plenty; I was where I wanted to be."

Casero paused again with a dreamy gesture, took a swig, then a drag on his cigarette, silence, a brief cough, and then he looked at Álvaro and went on with his story:

"They took almost everything, because that's what this business is like: The Lord giveth and the Lord taketh away. And whatever they left me, Charlie is collecting, not because morphine is so expensive, don't believe it, it's just that I can't buy from anybody else. You get that? It's a protected business, and I'm what they call a captive client. I've managed to keep my office till now, but soon that, too, will come to an end, and afterwards who knows, the wild dogs will show up. That's why I like this mess. I don't know if this will help us make your wife reappear; I hope so. I say this with all my heart, but I don't think there's any other way to find her. You have to plant a bomb in the middle of the square and blow everything to pieces. Only then is it possible someone'll say where they put Alicia. Go see Charlie and tell him I sent you; of course he'll collect in advance." Casero stubbed out his cigarette, pulled some papers from a drawer and handed them to him.

"Give him this," Casero said. "It's my last property title; that'll convince him of my good intentions. Tell him we can write up the mortgage tomorrow; it'll be enough for all the toys he's looking for and to buy me a few more of my vials for a while. Anyway, afterwards I won't repay even the first IOU, and he'll get to keep the apartment. That's how the game goes, and the truth is I don't give a shit; I'm already fucked. And, please, ask him to give you all the morphine he's got; tell him I'll settle up with him tomorrow. It doesn't matter—he'll beat the shit out of me, regardless. Before you take the tape, make me a copy... no, better make two copies, one for me and the other for my safety deposit box at the bank." Casero wrote something on a slip of paper.

"Here, this is the box number, just in case there's some witchcraft afoot. And speaking of witches, do you know who the black car belongs to?"

"The mayor?"

"Father Dupree."

6) LAS CASAS FM, THE VOICE OF THE PEOPLE

Charlie's computer was weighted down by several boxes, all of which had a seal reading "Department of Public Health, Los Huemules City Hospital: 2% morphine for medicinal use." In the warehouse there were gun belts, cameras, tripods, a large TV set underneath a microwave oven, a few CD readers, a telescope, some indescribable objects, VCRs, walkie-talkies and cell phones, cartons of imported cigarettes, boxes of liquor and wine (especially whiskey and champagne) and among them glimpses of compact packages of white powder.

"You're not very careful," Álvaro remarked. He was squatting and inspecting the PC.

"About what?" Charlie asked, thumbing through Casero's property title.

"Is that cocaine?" Álvaro nodded toward the packages.

"What's it to you?" Charlie had stopped between two pages and was staring at him.

"Nothing, I guess. Can I try this machine?"

"Sure. It works fine, but the customer has his rights. Why do you want it in such a hurry?"

"It's for a job. I have to digitize a video."

"What video?"

"It's private."

"I want to see it."

"You can't." Charlie looked up and dropped all the papers at Álvaro's feet.

"Take the papers, kid, and bring them to the shyster. I don't do any business I don't understand," Charlie replied as he stood to leave.

"It's something personal—what are you gonna see, huh? Me and my wife fucking?"

"I don't give a shit about your personal life, baby; I've got plenty of hookers in my life already, so I don't waste my time watching stupid shit, but if I don't know what's on that video, there's no deal. It's a simple as that."

Álvaro lowered his head and handed him the tape.

Charlie said: "I'll be with you in a little while. Meantime, connect your machine and see if it does you any good; make sure it's not something you'll want to return to me. The papers, please." He held out his hand, smiling agreeably.

Álvaro turned them over to him, and when the door swung closed, he sat down on the floor, trembling. He lit a cigarette and tried to calm down. Charlie was unpredictable, he thought: he was dirty enough to hand the tape over to Dupree, but he also saved room for his private dealings and he didn't ask questions, just as Casero had said. And yet, he had just asked him the worst, most unfortunate question possible. He decided there was no retake possible and prepared to get the machine ready. He rummaged around among pieces of equipment, found what he was looking for, connected it and tried it out. It was an acceptable machine, and even though the video card wasn't very fast, it had useful programs. He chose a VCR and left it attached to the equipment.

Charlie still hadn't returned. Álvaro lit another cigarette, looked for more devices, found some elements for jerry-rigging an edit island. That made him happy, but then he reproved himself for feeling that way when Alicia was still missing. Then he thought he might be doing something that would help find her, and he felt happy again. And after a while the cycle repeated.

Charlie still hadn't come back. Álvaro began to grow uneasy. He looked at the computer and felt ridiculous. A piece of equipment like that, ready to perform a task that would normally bring him pleasure—he was familiar with it from his experience with video clips; he had really enjoyed preparing those productions. And now he was anguished, he no longer felt confident about what he was doing and began to mull everything over: he had gotten involved in a strange place; he didn't like dangerous situations; his wife wasn't there; he was afraid to accept the possibility that she could be dead; he had no one to go to for help; and the lawyer was still his only support. He opened a box of morphine and took out a vial: it was just like the one he had seen at Casero's place. Inside the box was a pile of labels, held together with a rubber band: they were all labelled *Insulin* in typed letters.

Charlie opened the door. He looked like a man possessed.

"This is gonna cost you," he announced.

Álvaro turned pale.

"What do you mean, it's gonna cost me? I gave you the papers."

"Look, big shot, let's not even discuss the lawyer's rat trap. This stuff is worth a fortune. What else have you got?"

"I have my camera."

"Don't make me laugh. How much is your car worth?"

"Less than the camera."

Charlie thought for a moment, paced around the room a couple of times, and said:

"For starters, tell the shyster there's no more dope, not a single vial, and get me ten thousand dollars by tomorrow."

"There's no way. Please, don't do this to me," Álvaro begged.

"Listen to me, handsome, this is a very fucking tough situation," said Charlie, waving the video under Álvaro's nose. "You think you can buy me with a couple of pesos? Do you realize how risky this is for me? If it gets out that I'm making your work easier, I'll end up in the garbage dump. Your friend has resources; don't believe everything he says. When he runs out of candy, he'll make cash grow in the sand."

"My friend," Álvaro replied, slowly articulating each word, hearing himself say the word "friend," and speaking up for himself in a new way, a way that emerged from him spontaneously, "isn't going to get more money. His bankroll is gone and it's not a really good idea to screw around when a guy is at the end of his rope. You're trying to squeeze blood from a stone. It looks like bad business to me."

"Was that a threat?" Charlie asked with a charming smile.

"I'll lay it all out, just the way you like it, Chimp. I'm beginning to understand why they call you that. You can keep that video and show it to the big cheese or any of his ass kissers, but I have two copies. It's simple: I get out of here, hop into the car, and before you can pick up the phone, I'll be whizzing down the road, far from the hunters and wild dogs. And then, I swear, you're gonna have to get your shit together and do something with your life because things are about to turn very dark for you. You understand that, amigo?"

"And you'll leave your girl here?"

"What do you know about her?"

"I know lots of lovely things about this town."

"Where is she?"

"Not a clue, tiger, but there are other people who know."

"Who."

"Get me the ten grand." Charlie was looking at him.

Álvaro swallowed hard and turned red; his chest was a conga drum. He took a breath and spat out the words, "Is she alive?"

"The cash, baby, the cash."

7) A STRATEGIC CORNER RIGHT IN THE MIDDLE OF TOWN

Standing on the corner of the square, diagonally across from the bar and with his back toward the church, Álvaro was talking to Casero from a public phone, explaining what had happened with Charlie and looking around. People went by, and Álvaro noticed just how strange the town really was. Yes, of course, he saw the famous residents whom he had hardly noticed till now, the mothers who passed by, holding their unfortunate children by the hand. He saw an orange Traffic van, slowly driving along the avenue on the other side of the square, heading toward the church. The car overflowed with faces that smiled as if from another galaxy. Where could they be going? Álvaro wondered as he listened to the lawyer's voice on the other end of the line. Inside the Traffic, joyful faces pressed up against the spittle-coated windows, their eyes squinting as they surveyed the same, repetitive novelties that they jubilantly pointed out every day with their little fingers. The Traffic came close enough for Álvaro to read the writing on its flank: *Agnus Dei*, in happy, bubble-like letters.

A man of indeterminate age and serious expression came walking along the opposite sidewalk, greeting people, dogs, and telephone posts, stopping in front of the poster display at the movie house right next to the bar, diagonally across from where Álvaro stood. The posters had some meaning for him, Álvaro deduced, because the serious man gestured, a dramatic, decisive negative, turned around, greeted a telephone post and walked away in the opposite direction from the route he had taken to get there.

The mayor's wife walked by, too, as diminutive as ever, practically a dwarf, with her knitting equipment in a string bag from which bits of yarn and a pair of white needles emerged. She didn't even glance at Álvaro as she entered the church behind a woman wearing a white kerchief on her head.

The Traffic van had come to a halt, and now the orphans clambered out of the car, dispersed throughout the sandbox, arranged themselves in groups and began to play their games, which sometimes seemed obvious, like ring around the rosie, tag, and statues but which suddenly turned into odd rituals that never quite seemed to take shape. An assortment of flags made their appearance, the children formed groups, singing strange words in strange voices and laughing like the strange kids they were. Others, who had not been riding in the Traffic, began approaching; the sandbox filled with happy, bizarre faces. Still others, who were crossing the street, tugged at their mothers' hands, pulling them toward the sandbox; they managed to change the initial path and joined the games. There were multi-colored balloons, more incomprehensible chants—but they seemed to understand them, because they enjoyed them, laughing and squealing. A few Down Syndrome children came along and chatted vaguely with a couple of microcephalics, all of whom were adults, if it can be said that someone is ever truly an adult, and despite the differences in age, they joined together clumsily and approached the sandbox, picked up some flags and balloons, and sang along with the rest.

Despite the growing mayhem, Álvaro kept talking, watching the people and the time. He noticed how that strange group grew in number and in noise level; and how they kept dancing and humming under the severe gaze—always hidden beneath their peaked headdresses—of the nuns from the orphanage who cared for them, minding over them like watchdogs. Soon it would be dark, and Álvaro had nowhere to sleep. Go to the hotel, the lawyer said. It seemed like a bad idea to Álvaro. Go to the other hotel, Casero then suggested, but that recommendation was quashed, too; that place caused Álvaro intense anguish. Don't come to my office, the lawyer warned; it's not a good place to sleep anymore; there are vermin, understand? Álvaro didn't understand. A woman walked by holding the hand of a beautiful blonde little girl, as blonde as the sun. That reference to "vermin" must have a double meaning, Álvaro imagined, watching the lovely child's golden braids as she clung to her mother's hand, her exquisite white dress with its tiny blue-and-white flowers, her old-fashioned organdy collar. The child screamed and struggled, trying to bite the tree trunks, and the mother tugged on her hand; perhaps that very day, or another, not so distant one, she would end up ripping her arm from her shoulder. At last the child dragged her mother toward the sandbox, as the others had done before, managed to let go of her arm and devote herself to happily gnawing on a walnut tree. The orphans and their retinue sang, did handstands, danced in a circle, and played a sort of hopscotch without directions or access to heaven; fallen angels that they were, perhaps they weren't even interested in reaching a heavenly destination, reserved only for the genetically pure. And there was so much noise in the square, so much crazy confusion, that someone from the town stepped out onto the balcony, possibly to see what was going on. There was a sudden silence; as if guided by a single will, the little faces turned toward the balcony, while the flags and balloons remained, like mute witnesses of the abrupt vacuum that had been generated, floating above the multi-shaped heads. Álvaro fell silent, perhaps attracted by so much stillness, perhaps because of that unexpected feeling of modesty that occurs whenever everyone is quiet and one person keeps talking; their voice becomes more noticeable, as does the subject they're talking about, something like an intimacy suddenly exposed to the air, something that is concealed among the various voices when those voices are present.

The man who had appeared on the balcony seemed to know what to do: he waited even longer and the anticipation grew. Everyone had fallen silent, and for one moment the noise of the swings, the passing breeze, the distant echo of seagulls pecking away at the garbage dump three blocks away, could all be heard, as could the voice of the lawyer that still emanated from the phone and which seemed like the only sound—unauthorized—in that place, a faint, hesitant, metallic murmur. "What's going on?"asked Casero's tiny voice. "Shh," said Álvaro, covering the earpiece.

The man on the balcony, now the absolute commander of the scene, let another moment go by and at last smiled, opened his arms, greeted the children, and then shouts and laughter erupted, and the balloons and flags waved happily and everything returned to normal.

Álvaro took up the conversation again. "Tell me a place, then. I need a bed to sleep in. I'm not about to run risks for another night." And the lawyer suggested the orphanage. This struck Álvaro as ridiculous, and just as he was about to say so, an old woman collapsed beside him, foaming at the mouth, and nobody would help her. He reconsidered and thought that he should at least find out if it was possible to get some sort of private room. He was prepared to pay for it, to make a selfless contribution to the public good; what did the lawyer think? The lawyer thought it was a good idea; in any case, Mother Aurora was always there, and since they already knew one another, that made things easier, which was why Álvaro brought up another important topic, specifically if it was worthwhile to negotiate with Charlie, who had returned the video, though the fact was, he had already seen it, and that was a dangerous thing. "It doesn't matter," replied the lawyer; Charlie was sure he had him by the balls. "Had who?" Álvaro inquired, distracted by a kind of horizontal bicycle going by, in which the legless body of a vigorous, excessively hairy man lay. The man propelled himself along by activating a clever mechanical set-up with his two thick arms while singing "La Morocha."

"You," Casero replied. "And me, too. And, he *did* say that about your wife," Casero went on.

"Oh, sure, I understand," said Álvaro, watching two other nuns who were almost certainly heading for the orphanage with their gray habits, broad headdresses, and hidden faces. They went by chattering, like desert emanations in what sounded to him like another language.

"By the way," inquired Álvaro, remembering Father Dupree, "why does the priest say Mass in Latin? I thought that wasn't done anymore."

"Because he's conservative, reactionary, and pre-conciliar, of course, and his position is essentially a return to Christ, whatever that means," the lawyer hissed. "In any case, you should be paying attention to Father Dupree's worst nightmare right now."

"What are you referring to?" asked Álvaro.

"To the high degree of genetic pollution in this town, Alvaro. What you're seeing at this moment happens every day," Casero explained. And Álvaro was seeing it. Ayala was taking a spin around the square in his new police car, endowed with all the technical advantages necessary to guarantee the safety of the town's children. Maybe he had been referring to the children with more subtle—or even hidden—deformities, a different species, a privileged caste that would, when they became adults, join the army of recreational hunters who cleaned up the bad genes that had come from God knows which inferno. He knows where Alicia is, Álvaro reasoned, losing the thread of the conversation or picking it up again after looking into the eyes of Ayala, who at this precise moment was passing by very close to him. Taking his right foot off the gas, he stared back at Álvaro, hard—a warning stare, or so it seemed to him. Álvaro, who was sure, or nearly sure, he understood that gesture, mentioned it to Casero and asked if Charlie had told Ayala about the video yet.

"Could be, though that would put the whole business at risk, of course." It's just as likely he'd say something after receiving that money, which is why Casero thought they still had some time, and anyway it was true that he, Casero, had resources. He could get the money, but he couldn't pay it back. In short, these were tough times: Mother Aurora could give him a loan. It was a delicate matter, and he suggested that Álvaro hold off on telling her about any of this if he was determined to ask her for refuge, and...

"You know something?" Casero asked first and then answered immediately, "If they come looking for you there, it's likely they won't be able to get in, because nothing is supposed to happen without her permission, and Father Dupree isn't prepared to break into her headquarters, so it's not a bad idea to stay close to that place and wait. It's one thing," the lawyer explained, "to kidnap a child, and quite another to charge in with fire and sword; it's a slight exaggeration, but it's like I'm telling you." Álvaro thanked him, touched by the information the lawyer had provided. He no longer had any doubts; he hung up and headed for the orphanage.

{XI}
SANCTUS

1) THE WARNINGS

The mural of the inferno held details that branched out and re-
sulted in new details, creating a treelike structure where synthe-
sis seemed impossible, a weave containing hidden revelations,
which, as the eye explored its angles, nooks, and crannies, led
to yet other new scenes that contained, along the borders or
through subtle changes in perspective, other previous, simul-
taneous, or subsequent moments, like brief, inserted anecdotes,
constantly occurring in the background, but acquiring meaning only upon their discovery. Some of them gave meaning to
others, or gained meaning from earlier scenes, creating panora-
mas before the viewer's eyes that unfolded in a stillness saturat-
ed with movement, inviting further exploration, which delayed
the observer and could hold him back without a clear sense of
how much time had gone by:

A man with closed eyes, in a posture that could be inter-
preted either as religious passion or extreme suffering, chained
to the burning wooden mast of a ship, grimaced agonizingly
while being punished by an avenging figure that became increasingly enraged with the poor wretch, thrusting a dagger—
one more in a series of daggers already inserted—into the tor-

tured man's belly. The daggers, well-honed and sharp, bore an inscription on their blades: *confutatis maledictis*. Next to the suffering soul's head, on a pictorial plane behind and apart from him, another scene was developing: an enormous egg broke open, and from its interior emerged a serpent with sinister red eyes, opening its mouth to sink its fangs into an innocent-looking goat. Black, winged creatures, possibly bats, sprung from the goat's mouth, flew toward a nearby tower, and hid among the battlements. On the balcony of that same tower, a woman—dark-skinned and desirable, with vaguely indigenous eyes and straight, dark hair that cascaded over her shoulders—smiled and looked downward, where a recently-fallen male figure lay on his back, his arms still raised toward her. The trace of a lewd expression of frustrated craving could still be detected on his face: possibly the hapless victim had tumbled after a thwarted attempt to penetrate that fortress, perhaps after attaining it. The woman's smile didn't suggest a virginal expression, but rather one tinged with a sort of malice. Below the horizon, in a hole where the fires burned and on a different plane, a demonic figure—whose face resembled those of the orphans playing on the orphanage's patio—laughed insatiably. Higher up and beyond the inferno, two fair-skinned angels kept watch from the heavens and witnessed the proceedings with tears of sorrow over the unhappy destiny of God's creatures. The angels' expressions looked like those of someone who inflicts a dreadful punishment on a beloved child and suffers the pain of wounding the flesh of his flesh. It looked as though the fallen man at the foot of the tower and the man who was martyred by the demon were really one and the same, guilty of the sin of fornication. Perhaps he had died after that encounter with the woman, and that was why he was already in hell, paying for his sins. It was logical to think that she had pushed him, and if that was the case, then it was a matter of murder, something shocking for a mural painted in a church building. It seemed like the woman had the upper hand; one might deduce that she must have participated actively in the seduction. Her obvious expression and her disheveled hair suggested it: a hellhound, unpunished.

What was undeniable was that the warning could be found in the tortures administered and in the personification of the devil, who controlled the action with his face of an unrepentant beast and his slanted eyes. The devil's tongue, fat and dripping, stuck out of his mouth in an easily recognizable gesture.

2) BLOW AND GO

Álvaro entered the orphanage late in the afternoon. It was recess, so the orphans were running around everywhere, playing their games and dancing. Escorted by the stone-faced nun on duty, he walked among seas of abandoned children and nuns who came and went, issuing orders and keeping the students in line: some of the children clustered around him, regaling him with their most raucous laughter, stroking and embracing him with hands tinted the most ignoble colors and indefinable substances that thickened their skin and erased their nails. They kissed him with damp, generous lips; they licked his cheeks, bestowing their fetid breath upon him, the most indescribable smells emanating from their chubby bodies. They begged for reciprocity, candies, news from the outside world; they asked if their unlikely mama was baking them a birthday cake, what the house where they had never lived was like; his name and how old he was. They also asked his mother's name. Anastasia, Álvaro replied, the first name he could think of. He wanted to run away; he took one step and the question came up again. This time it was Manuela; later it would be Josefina. Others, however, treated him with an indifference that Álvaro was silently grateful for.

And now, standing before the infernal mural, under Christ's attentive gaze, he waited to be received by the Mother Superior. Álvaro was trying to undo the knots and webs of the more-or-less concealed allusions communicated by that painting with Renaissance pretentions when the door swung open and he was ushered into Mother Aurora's dark hall. The nun was seated in her wheelchair, her back toward the door, staring out a window that faced the patio to which the forsaken children were now heading for recess.

"Come closer," the woman invited him.

He walked over and stood beside her, gazing at the patio. The woman wasn't about to shift her gaze, and Álvaro didn't feel he had the authority to turn her around and speak to her face to face, so they spoke without looking at one another, except for some furtive glances on his part, whenever the nun was answering his questions. There was one memory: it was a kermesse. Álvaro was holding his father's hand; they had stopped in front of a place where there was a woman's head placed on top of something that his memory insisted on remembering as a flower pot, thought it might have been a tiny box. Álvaro had squeezed his father's hand, unable to keep his eyes on that sight, and searching for someplace to rest his gaze, he went from that incongruous head to the other spectators and then back to the woman, but just for a moment: it was unbearably attractive, a sweet martyrdom he could not ignore. Álvaro neither looked nor turned away. The horrifying image became less atrocious when the woman, or rather her head, smiled at the public as the master of ceremonies touted the extraordinary miracle of that female body stuck inside a flowerpot—which might have been a tiny box—as well as that lady's incredible gift for predicting the future.

"Step right up and see," announced the man, who, Álvaro seemed to recall, wore a yellow top hat. "Step right up and see the marvelous Sybil," he invited them over his loudspeaker. "Learn your future, find out what destiny has in store for you. The Sybil will tell you, step right up and see, ladies and gentlemen, come in and see."

They didn't enter the booth. Despite his father's insistence, Álvaro refused: That vision, suspended in time, was a troubling power that returned every so often. The memory also included a fact that was repeated: Now Álvaro didn't look at Mother Aurora's face. Instead, he was distracted—though he couldn't see them—by the actions of the young orphans down below.

"Why did you come?" the Mother Superior asked.

"I have nowhere to sleep," Álvaro replied.

"They're already looking for you."

"I'm not sure; it's possible. I think I did something stupid. They might know that I have proof."

"What proof?" The head remained motionless, the eyes glued to her orphans.

"I made a video of the hunt. It shows the police chief driving the black car."

"Did anyone see you?" the nun asked.

"Charlie. I went to see him to work out a system to improve the visuals, because the recording isn't very clear, and Casero said that it wasn't enough to help him prove anything. And then he told me that Charlie was very discreet, but he insisted on seeing the tape, and I had no choice. When he saw it, he asked for more money, and I'm not sure he won't rat me out anyway."

"How much did he ask for?"

"A lot, ten thousand dollars," said Álvaro with a hint of uneasiness as he recalled that Casero had advised him to be discreet in this regard and leave the money negotiations to him.

"That's not the problem. But he's going to point a finger at you, anyway; I don't think it makes sense to pay him. You shouldn't hang around here. My advice is for you to leave town with that tape and do whatever you need to do far away from here."

"Someone else already gave me advice like that."

"Who?"

"El Tolo. He says it isn't safe here."

"El Tolo, I see. He probably told you about the trips to the desert," the nun speculated.

"No."

"In the past, some twenty years ago, maybe more, they didn't finish off my children; they stuck them in the trunk of the black car and took them away, still alive, unconscious or close to death, and when they reached the desert, they left them there. People said that it was a way of releasing them into the hands of God, like in the old trials by ordeal; if any one of them survived, that meant that he was pure in spirit, even if he had a genetic defect, and that was why God let him live. But if he was dead by daybreak, if his remains were devoured by the dogs, the Inquisitorial theory was confirmed. They continued doing all that according to strict instructions left by Jean Dupree in his manual: in the desert, God decides; write that in Gothic letters so everyone will understand it perfectly. It's a twisted thing to explain; it seems incomprehensible these days, but those things do happen, even in the most advanced countries. I don't believe culture changes anything; these are phenomena that happen all the time, one way or another, and young people or children tend to be the constant targets. In the story of the Holy Innocents, there's an annihilation that comes from certain prophecies and only serves to keep Herod, a paranoid king, in power. Here, in a different context, the same story took place, the idea of a necessary massacre floated above the town, and the people kept quiet; some of them decided not to say anything, and others justified it, more or less silently. If you insist, from the pulpit, on the idea of a silent, secret war, if you denounce the lukewarm observers and praise the supposed combatants who claim to risk their lives for a greater cause, in the end people will accept your arguments, out of apathy or sympathy. They'll also keep silent out of fear, because no one is exempt from birthing deformed children. The children had no way to organize a defense; the dogs or the cold killed them. But that was in the beginning, a simple exercise in extermination, something hard to sustain without breaking the will of the hit men themselves. Which is exactly what happened to El Tolo. He couldn't take it anymore: he saw the insanity mixed in with politics and he felt abandoned. He was a warrior of God. He had clung to the idea that they were fighting for something greater, that it was the way to preserve traditions and put an end to the beatings administered to those ill-born children, but to let them die in such a sordid way was too much for him. I'm not making excuses for him, I'm just saying that he believed that murder carried out for a just cause wasn't murder, but rather reparations; it was a way to move forward based on a supreme ideal, to cleanse the blood. He's still a son-of-a-bitch, with apologies to bitches everywhere, but now nobody respects him. Eventually they gave all that up to make way for something more consistent: now they hunt them down, because hunting has its own mystique, but in the end they finish them off: They're 'humanitarian'; it's a merciful gesture, and everything became more secretive because of a matter of formality, but not too much so. And besides, nobody believes that the wild dogs are God's guardians or some other bullshit like that."

Álvaro remained silent for a moment.

"Where did those dogs come from?" he asked.

"They were big-game hunting dogs, but the breed degenerated in the desert. They were wild even then; now they're more dangerous than jaguars. In Jean Dupree's time they used them to hunt huemules, which was a perfectly legal sport, a popular form of entertainment. Much later, the huemules were exterminated or left the area, and it was never clear why the dogs stayed in the desert. They just left them there, and for some reason they never came back. There's no stopping them, or else nobody cares. It's another reason not to go out at night. But it's easier in the daytime. Go home, Álvaro, there's nothing to be done here."

"You're throwing me out."

"I'm suggesting that you do what's safest for you."

"I can't go: I don't know anything about my wife yet. That video might help. Casero has a copy."

Mother Aurora didn't respond; she stared out at the patio. A bell rang, and the nuns went out to round up the children. It was quite a spectacle to behold: at least twenty sisters, indistinguishable from one another, like a little army of nuns, running behind the students, who, unwilling to be captured, struggled, hid, and engaged in all sorts of capers to flee from their wardens, shrieking with glee or fright.

"Does that look familiar to you?" the Mother Superior asked.

"They look like they're used to it. Do they play at being hunted?"

"The kids always play, and these children are kids forever. They're so docile... it's a question of kindness and good treatment. That's how they're carried off—playing. By the way, Casero asked me to do an investigation. I wasn't able to find out too much, but what I see from here is that Anselmo is missing. He was thirteen, microcephalic. It must be him. Is he in your film?" the nun inquired.

"Dead and very fuzzy. But I saw him close up. Short, chubby, he looked older; he was wearing a yellow sweatshirt, he limped a little. I have something, I think."

Mother Aurora didn't reply, and Álvaro watched her: Tears streamed down her face, and no part of her moved: the bust of a weeping head, the women from the kermesse, frozen and with the ancient gesture modified. The nun was a pythoness that could read the past.

"When did your wife disappear?"

"Monday night."

"That's when Fermín and Lucila went missing. Did you look for her?"

"Wherever I could. I asked at the places you told me to."

"I'm asking you if you looked for her, not if you went through channels."

Álvaro felt a stab of anguish.

"No."

"Then you have to do that."

"How?"

"I don't know. Go for a walk, sniff around discreetly. Go out at night, If you hear running, get away, and try not to tangle with the dogs. It's not easy, but you have good reason to take risks."

"Am I looking for my wife's body?"

"Look at it that way, Álvaro; this has never happened here

before. I can't imagine that they're holding her somewhere. Why would they have kidnapped her? And when they find out about your video, things will move faster. I don't think it'll go on much longer. If you want to stay here, you can sleep in the tower, but you have to understand that this isn't a sanctuary. It's a fact someone's going to talk. And they *will* come after you."

"Casero says that Dupree doesn't break into his own headquarters."

"It's true, but you've changed the rules. In any case, Charlie won't do anything till the money shows up."

"But he could rat me out and collect the money anyway. As long as I don't know about it, he takes the money and then they come after me."

"It doesn't matter; they're going to wait for you, anyway. I don't think they want to ruin the deal. He leaves everybody dividends; that'll give you a little time. How soon does he want that money?"

"By tomorrow."

"I'll give you part of it. Go see him and explain that you're collecting the rest. Try to buy time. And let's hope he bites. Come with me."

Using her mouth, Mother Aurora picked up a tube that was lying next to her cheek, connected to a motor in back of the wheelchair. She blew into it once, the chair made a buzzing sound and moved in reverse.

"I'll help you, Mother."

"No need; this works quite well." She kept blowing and maneuvering; she rolled over to the desk and indicated a drawer. Álvaro opened it and found a bundle of dollars. It looked like a lot of money.

"There's enough there; take half. Charlie will drool over it; he may even wait. In any case, I urge you to use that money and not forget why I'm giving it to you. Press that button, please."

Álvaro pressed the button and a nun—a different one or the same one as before—appeared. The Mother Superior gave her some instructions and wished Álvaro a good night.

"It's early," Álvaro said.

Mother Aurora cut him short. "Get some rest. And no matter what, don't turn on the light in the tower."

2) A BRIGHT NIGHT IN A DARK TOWER

But Álvaro couldn't rest. Not that night, or the ones after that, because a person rests only when he can let time flow by; tomorrow we'll take up our normal activities again; it's a well-known fact that there can be rest only when there's no reason to wonder about life, or at least, about the body, no trace of the corpse of the woman he loves, or to stop and wonder if he's committed so many stupid acts as to have put her at risk: to childishly trust the mythical power of the Chevy, for example, capable of undergoing a forced march with no water, no oil, and—why not?—no gas, and to trust the lawyer's (obviously mistaken) advice to do business with an immoral dealer like Charlie, and also to think that church properties are inviolable, despite Mother Aurora's warning; or to trust Charlie to keep mum in order to keep his business safe, which made Álvaro begin to fear that it would cost him his life, which might not be so important, he thought; there's no underestimating a beaten man, he had told Charlie, believing it was the right moment to leave—another bit of naiveté, and he tossed and turned in the cot, looked out the window of the tower, and the stars were high in the sky; you could barely detect the glow of the moon outside the window frame, right there, the moon, as if keeping watch over the procession of the stars, the vault of heaven, watching the space abandoned by the sun, as it has done every night since the world began. When Álvaro was finally able to rest, and his heavy sleep was calm, he dreamed so deeply and sweetly and he so loved that dream, which nourished his thoughts and offered him nearly complete film scripts on awakening, and because of that love, perhaps, because it had been an inexhaustible treasure, the most precious treasure of all, he hadn't even been disturbed when Alicia left the unfamiliar bed of the unfamiliar desert hotel named for a sea bird; yes, she got up and he kept sleeping and there was no more Alicia and who knows if there ever would be again, what had become of her, she had to be somewhere, in chains and waiting for him to come and free her, waiting for the Álvaro of Álvaro's road movie, for his dry, snakeskin steps in shoes with taps, for his .38 with its 13 notches on the mother-of-pearl handle, and his knife, sharp enough to cut a high wire cable. Álvaro asked himself these questions and felt stupid, like a hopeless fool, but in spite of everything, he let himself be carried away by the questions in his dreams: there she'd be, hiding, playing a sinister game, waiting for the right moment to pop out, perhaps to teach him a lesson for his stupidity and his naiveté, and in that case, what would it matter now that he was involved in a different, more sinister game, believing he was searching for her. Álvaro felt like a tough guy who had just invented another tough guy who knew what to do in any situation, because knowing what to do was always a matter of the time required by the film script, and if you didn't find the solutions today, you'd find them tomorrow or next month, so what was he doing there, in that dark, cold tower from which he could see nearly the whole town, and also, two blocks away, the building that had belonged to Casero when his glory was intact, with its single light turned on, indicating that the lawyer was in his office, perhaps dreaming his morphine dream. Maybe owning the only pair of tall buildings in a tiny town had some mysterious clout that had linked Casero with Aurora, two disabled beings, after all: she, the head, and he, the lame man, a strange pair that didn't really know where they were leading him, Álvaro, who was allied with these people, trusted them, and maybe that was just another sign of his naiveté, *confutatis maledictis*, another way of believing in Santa Claus, in the invincible resilience of his mythical coupe, another knife in his belly, now that he was lying in a strange, empty, bed, in a tower that well might have been the one he'd seen in the mural of the inferno—the only thing missing was for the tousled-haired, unpunished brunette to appear and thrust him into the arms of a snarling demon. At least it was clear that Aurora wouldn't be that woman; that was progress, anyway, and after a while he fell asleep.

Or maybe he nodded off for a moment and opened his eyes and saw the stars in their proper place, but it could certainly be possible that they'd moved—what did Álvaro know of the desert stars in the southern part of the world, nothing, and so he stood up and looked out the window, but the moon was high, and he had clearly slept, but not rested, because when you sleep with a powerful idea in your head, on awakening you realize that your sleep had been feverish and fitful; you open your eyes and it's as if everything was still there: you slept, yes, but you didn't dream; your kept thinking as though in a delirium, wondering in your sleep about your naiveté, and it's a sharp, painful way of interrogating yourself or of sleeping, going round and round the same subject with no resolution, pounding away at the same questions and trying to squeeze some juice from your thoughts that will never flow because thoughts are made of stone and pain, of remorse and an impossible desire to turn back the clock and start over, this time avoiding mistakes and foolishness, a torture which, in the long run, is capable of leaping crazily around the same subject forever, repeating questions and their impossible solutions, returning with relief, as in nightmares, to abandoned places, saying "I've arrived," but knowing at the same time that you're back at the starting point, that is, that nothing changed during that brief lapse, like the stars outside the window, which nevertheless had moved; there were other stars and other starlight, but no rest, your body could attest to that, your body that still ached from those feverish days of which this scanty dream was an example.

He looked down and noticed activity on the patio, and since the moon was bright, he could see a handover taking place: an anonymous nun held two children by the hand. They crossed the patio that faced the front door, bathed in the leprous glow of the moon. It must have been three AM. The children proceeded obediently toward the green door; the green door opened; a dark-colored car with its lights on waited behind them; the black silhouettes of three sturdy men were outlined by the car's headlights. The children stood on tiptoe to reach the nun's dark cheek, as she leaned over to make it easier for them. They placed their faces inside the shadowy reach of the headdress, gave her a damp goodnight kiss, and now walked away holding the men's hands. They might have been smiling. The green front door swung closed.

Álvaro didn't hesitate. He ran downstairs, taking two or three steps at a time, spinning like a wheel of fortune. He was going to catch that perfidious nun; once and for all someone was going to pay for the misery those children had been plunged into and the atrocity of handing them over to the hunters. As he continued down the stairs, he bumped against the rounded sides of the tower, steadying himself as best he could because there were no handrails and the light was dim. Like the lewd man in the mural of the inferno, Álvaro underestimated the possibility of falls. Seized by righteous anger, panting and shouting, he knew in some dark recess of his conscience that the moment to act had just vanished with the departure of the children. It was late, and perhaps it was even reprehensible to pursue a cowardly act of justice. He reached the ground floor and turned around: to his right, he managed to spy the nun who had handed the children over slipping down a corridor from the other side of the patio, and he ran in that direction. The corridor was long, and in the distance he could make out the figure of the nun, who was rapidly walking away. He didn't hesitate to charge after her, which made the nun stop and turn, and Álvaro could discern a look of alarm in the darkness of her hidden face. His footsteps had alerted her, and he decided it was too late for regrets, so he went on: clumsy, foolish, and now cowardly; it was the moment to run the guilty party down, at the very least. He gained distance, because no woman can run as fast as a duped man, least of all this woman in her uncomfortable habit; he caught up somewhat, but the nun didn't stop. Then Álvaro called her, "Come here, Sister, don't be frightened. I want to talk to you," but the treacherous nun fled, lifting her skirts and speeding up. She maintained the distance between them, turned right, entered another corridor; four strides and Álvaro was there behind the nun, who now, just a few yards away, slipped into her room and closed, but didn't lock, the door. Álvaro clearly noted her carelessness, and, influenced perhaps by his film scripts or by his dreams, wondered as he ran if he might be heading for a trap, but even if he was, nothing mattered to him anymore. Armed with resolve, he advanced urgently toward the oak door, grabbed the door handle, and opened it. He entered a hall with long benches and an atrium in the rear. A small crowd in gray habits, with broad headdresses and hidden faces turned toward him when he burst into the room where all the nuns in the orphanage were getting ready for morning prayers.

$\{$XII$\}$
BENEDICTUS

1) THE HORNS OR THE TAIL

By morning he had it all decided: first of all, he would negotiate with Charlie; later, when he had his hands on something concrete, he would consult Casero; and finally, maybe that very day or the next if he had made head or tail out of anything, he would see Dupree. He was the true objective of this whole thing; Álvaro would have to bring him something more solid. If he managed to process the tape, they were going to have to negotiate. He was prepared to hand it over in exchange for information about Alicia. The important thing was to buy time; though he still didn't see where all this was leading, he knew that time was essential. He left the orphanage early. The nun who walked him to the door didn't speak. He walked behind her, as usual. He considered the risk involved in the previous night's episode: he might have been running after this same nun, who knows, and in any case, what difference did it make if she was or wasn't the same one. The one he had pursued, that one, at least, was the traitor the Mother Superior was looking for, so that woman had to have talked, he concluded. The risk was definite; there was no room for naïveté.

He walked around the block, heading toward the radio

station. When he passed the church, he stopped for a second and his plans changed: the little bit of extra time he'd been begging for didn't mean a thing. He decided that Charlie and his business deals could go to hell. He had a copy of the recording, he had the number of the P.O. box where another copy was kept, and, most importantly, Casero had the third.

He entered the church. His thoughts were racing faster than he could comprehend. No one was praying; something felt strange. He went over to the confessional, entered, and sat down to wait. After a while, the wooden cover moved and the priest's face peeked out from behind the latticed opening.

"Forgive me, Father, for I have sinned."

"What have you done?"

"I've lost my wife."

"Have you done anything to make that happen?"

"I forgot to put water in the radiator."

"I'm afraid I don't understand." The priest's harsh voice revealed a state of alert.

"The engine overheated and the piston rod broke. I had to sleep at a hotel in town. When I woke up, my wife wasn't next to me and I haven't had any news about her since then."

"That's not a sin."

"Of course not, and I also taped the hunt for Anselmo."

"I see." The priest cleared his throat.

"And Chief Ayala shows up very clearly, Father. In any case, there are unmistakable images of this town and of a black car that they keep at El Tolo's house, a former soldier of God."

"This doesn't sound like a confession," the priest said at last.

"But it is, and to be frank, I hope you'll accept it as such, because I'm negotiating with you, and if you have a shred of dignity, you won't be bastard enough to break the Confessional seal, Father, because that's a sacrilege, I think, and if it's not, it's shitty behavior from someone who says Mass in Latin and declares himself the savior of his town's pure blood. Don't forget the recordings, dear Father. I want to know where my wife is!" said Álvaro, practically shouting.

"Silence, we're in a holy place," exhorted Dupree, and it wasn't a lie.

"You're right, Father," Álvaro went on, trying to lower the volume of the voice he felt emerging of its own accord, "but I don't give a damn about you and the motherfuckers who kiss your ass; they're a bunch of murderers disguised as saints. You're worse than Satan and all his legions; you're the demons, Father, not the poor wretches you kill every night, and don't forget that my tapes are well guarded, I'm not shitting you, and I'm tired of people messing with my ass. I want to know where my wife is!" Álvaro exploded, his voice echoing throughout the church, having by now lost the wavering composure of the beginning. He was trembling, ready to burst through the latticed opening and strangle the priest. He noticed the pigeons fluttering up above, at the top of the cupola.

"You're blaspheming. I think the situation merits speaking elsewhere."

"Right here's just fine with me."

"Elsewhere," the priest demanded, rising to his feet. "Follow me."

As they left the confessional, three women with white kerchiefs on their heads turned toward Álvaro, who followed the priest to a side door and into Dupree's office.

"Have a seat," Dupree said, pointing to a chair facing his desk.

Álvaro sat and lit a cigarette with Alicia's Zippo.

"Please don't smoke," Dupree urged.

"Don't worry about my health, Father. When I finish the cigarette, I'll light up another one with the stub of this one. I'm going to keep smoking till we're done talking."

"You've got the wrong enemy," the priest began to explain. "We're not responsible if something happened to your wife; nobody around here knows anything about her. And don't think I haven't heard about your case; it's very difficult for anyone to hide something from me. You're dealing with enough information to know that. In my opinion, you've taken the wrong path and filled yourself with questions that don't concern you. Most likely your wife saw something she shouldn't have seen, but what happened there was different from what you assume. It could be that when she witnessed that terrible scene, she tried to run away; anyone would be frightened to see what your wife saw. It's not a sight for sensitive souls; things were happening there that only armed men can tolerate. I myself never attend those happenings because I'm a godly man; I insist on having my instructions obeyed. Killing one's enemy is a human act, but only those who are prepared should carry it out. No pope ever fought in the Crusades, so why should I? To do that you need be of a different mettle. It makes sense to think that she was terrified because she didn't understand what she was seeing, and she took the wrong path. They tell me she ran toward the desert; from that point her fate is out of my hands."

"Sure, in the desert she's in the hands of God. It's all very Biblical. And you people are the moral storehouse of humanity. I get it: we're facing a crusade of the misunderstood, who don't stop and ask for support to fulfill their destinies. Am I on the right track, Father?" replied Álvaro, sucking furiously on his cigarette.

"Not too bad, but I don't see where you're going with this."

"Father, my wife was at the hospital that night; Romano brought her there. Stop lying to me, I beg you. I'm not in the mood for fairy tales."

As promised, Álvaro lit the second cigarette with the stub of the previous one, then looked for an ashtray and, not finding one, ground it out on the polished wooden floor.

The priest seemed surprised. He drummed his fingers on the desk.

"Do you have proof of that?"

"All thought leads to turbulence, Father; those are your words. You also said that nobody gets out of here alive. Those are hard words. Who's going to open his mouth? And, anyway, we haven't reached the trial stage yet, so let's not talk about proof. Accept my theory and let's see where it leads us."

"Tell it to me."

"You people went too far, Father, that's what I think. She saw them hunt down Fermín and Lucila; those were their names. I mention it in case you don't have that information. Alicia went out into the street and confronted them, because that's how she is—my wife is very passionate—and I can imagine the scene: she goes out and throws herself on them, and she's not satisfied with harsh words: she goes and fights. My wife is capable of beating them up without paying too much attention to how big they are or what kinds of weapons they have, and it's even likely she'd place herself between those poor children and the hunters' shotguns. The ones who were there were Romano, Tanco and Mainieri; there might have been someone else, but Romano wasn't the one who fired. I don't think it was Tanco, either, though I'm not saying he didn't want to. You must've seen how that old piece of shit looked at my wife's tits, and then there was Mainieri, who has a loose trigger finger. They say it's because he's reckless and an asshole, but I think there's a greater perversity at work here, so let 's say it was Mainieri who shoots and wounds her. How am I doing? It's just a theory, Father; I don't know how seriously he wounded her, and maybe it wasn't critical. No doubt Tanco looks the other way and Romano bawls him out, like a strict mother. Then they pick her up, toss her into the black car, and take her to the hospital, where they try to help her, but they didn't do anything because there was nothing to do, or for some other reason I still don't understand. So then they left, but I don't know where they went. After a while Ayala came by, saying he was making rounds, and, Father Dupree, you're going to have to accept my allegation that a Chief of Police doesn't make rounds at night, even in a shithole town like this. What was your Chief of Police doing at the hospital, Father? Did he go there to make sure all was in order? Did he want to know if anyone had asked questions? Did he go to scare the witnesses? Can you tell me? And I'm puzzled about something else: I wonder, before all that happened, if they raped her. It wouldn't surprise me if Tanco did, and such excesses occur during wartime; every soldier chooses his booty, even if it's a holy war. It's probably the way the Lord chooses to pay well-deserved bonuses. In case you don't know it, your warriors of God are fooling you; it's a hypothesis I find very seductive because it has to do with your decadence, but to be honest with you, I wasn't born yesterday, Father: I think you're a liar, too. Things like that don't happen in Las Casas without your finding out about them. And I don't want to forget about your son. Casero doctored up the papers, but not the people's memory, and in spite of everything, some of them are capable of spreading the word about your acts of fraud."

Dupree looked as though he was about to explode: he was all red and still drumming his fingers. He stood up, went to the library, and brought over a book that he laid on the desk: *De Verum Naturae* was the title. And there was a long subtitle in Gothic letters:

A Treatise on Demonology, an illustrated natural history of Satan and his legion of aborted babies, of his heavenly origin as an angel of light, of his betrayal of God and his subsequent fall, of infernal categories of princes and other nobility, of their guises and lies, and the disguises the Enemy uses to penetrate the hearts of the pure.

Written below that were the author's name and the publication date:

Jean Dupree, 1743, Basel, Switzerland.

Álvaro glanced at it quickly: there were the forsaken children of the town, the chubby faces of the orphans, but with devil's spittle dripping from evil smiles and pointy skulls, wild eyes, mixed with goat's hooves, Janus-like faces, threatening derrières, and other curses of the Lord. He dropped the book with a cynical smile. This priest was really as crazy as a loon.

"I never lie, you impertinent young man; you should know that," Dupree said. "Casero's word, on the other hand, is meaningless. He can testify that that mentally deficient child is my son; I'll own up to it right here, and if he thinks that fact discredits me, then he's wrong again, because what he has to say isn't worth one cent. He still doesn't understand who I am. Nevertheless, I think there's a certain logic to his reasoning. I can detect the possible trickery of some scoundrel in his tale, and I assure you it won't go unpunished. Because this isn't a farce. You can take it with the seriousness it deserves or make fun of it, but here, in these pages, is the real reason; this is why we do it. Even if the world is blind, we have our eyes wide open." Dupree drummed on the thick volume with his right index finger.

"You're changing the subject; now you want to sell me your Gospel. Do you really think I'm interested in this mumbo jumbo? I didn't come here to find out what you and your crazies think or to stick my nose into your romantic escapades. As far as I'm concerned, you could be the father of all the inbred kids in the world. The only thing it shows is that your blood isn't so pure, either, and frankly it's not my problem. What I think is that this madness has to stop. I may fall with the rest of you, but it's out of our control now: the tapes will end up where they belong so all this will fall back on you. They're on their way. It still depends on me, but not for much longer. If something should happen to me, sooner or later someone will see them," Álvaro lied, somewhat carried away, wondering if he was taking the bull by the horns or the tiger by its tail.

"Do you get what I'm saying, or do you think I've come here in the name of the devil? Don't give me fairy tales, just tell me what your brother did with my wife, and maybe I'll calm down," Álvaro said with clenched teeth and trying to contain his distress. His mind filled up with images of himself leaping upon the old man, hanging him, hitting him with that stupid book till he broke his skull, stabbing him with the infernal daggers, stepping on his face. The priest didn't defend himself.

"My brother's an idiot, or haven't you noticed that yet? He can't even stand up. All he does is satisfy his gluttony; he's a piece of garbage that grows and grows, endlessly. It's a family stigma that embarrasses me and forces me to continue my struggle to the end. And I hope he dies soon, for everybody's good. He's a lost sheep, but he's a Christian and he's my blood. That's the only reason why I put up with him. Understand this, young man: in this town, I am God."

After a silence, Dupree raised his voice in a gloomy tone:

"Even if outsiders come, this isn't going to stop because it depends entirely on me. Here I'm the one to decide who lives and who dies, according to my own will. There's nowhere to go for help; no one will hear your call; this thing is completely in my hands up to the line where the desert begins. Beyond that point, God speaks; the dogs are his instruments. All this you see is something superior and transcendent, and it's clear you don't understand the extent of what we're experiencing. You're still very far off the mark, hopelessly lost. You're a deaf man who's arrived at a party by mistake and can't understand what the dancers are doing."

He ended his explanation, opened a desk drawer, took out a cardboard box, and pushed it toward Álvaro.

"Is this your instrument of justice?"

Álvaro was astonished. He took the box and opened it, trembling. There were the two tapes.

"What happened to Casero?" he managed to ask, and the trembling grew stronger.

"He's in God's hands."

2) DEATH AND FREEDOM

He didn't understand how he was able get up afterward, go to the door of Dupree's office, open it, cross the threshold, walk through the entire church and into the street without the priest attempting to stop him. It had been a very strong blow, and yet he was still alive and standing. And the surprising part of being alive was that, before he left, and no longer holding back his words or being clearly aware of what he was saying, he had announced he wasn't done yet, that he wasn't some idiot as the priest thought, and that he was about to receive a few surprises. What surprises could he give that medieval monster? He had been clinging to the video he still kept in his jacket, but it seemed more like a message in a bottle than an instrument of justice. Threatening the priest with surprises was like sitting down and waiting for them to come looking for him.

He walked straight ahead, not daring to cross the street. That made no sense, but the curb seemed like an inaccessible divider, and the mere idea of getting close to it began to fill him with dread. So he veered left, walking slowly, like an old man. He saw the bar where Romano was drinking his gin beside Ayala, and the two of them watched him; farther along, Mainieri stood guard at the door of the police station, and he, too, watched him. Tanco arrived on his bicycle and stopped when he saw Álvaro. El Tolo parked the pickup next to the town hall, watched Álvaro pass by, and, having nothing to say to him anymore, closed the door—Álvaro heard the distant sound like a click drawn out by the wind—headed for the bar, went inside, sat down with Ayala and Romano, ordered a gin, and joined the group of observers. With ten eyes on the back of his head, Álvaro turned the corner, walking hesitantly toward the orphanage. He was knocked out, unstable: if there were any ropes in the ring, he no longer knew where they were. Someone needed to throw in the towel; he was alone and confused, and they were going to kill him.

He walked the whole block, thinking you can't escape a gaze; you're lucky if you can even get out of focus. And if you walk slowly, it's possible the gazers won't miss a certain detail. The detail was this: a young man, shabby looking, in a black leather jacket that lent him a certain dignity thanks to the nobility of the leather itself, not because of who was wearing it, walking slowly and as if it hurt him to put his feet down, moving the skinny mass of his body from one point to another, with his hands in his pockets, his hair dirty and in disarray, and his head bent, carefully monitoring the ground where he took his painful steps. He could sense a vague tremor, though it was more an inference than a verification: it wasn't that he was trembling, but rather that he was done for, and in any case, the trembling he sensed was like that of a wounded animal that knows the final blow will arrive at any moment, the full awareness that it's living the moment just before the end, the moment of surrender, convinced that there's nothing left to do; the struggle has ended and the survival instinct, if such a thing exists, has gathered up its possessions and left, because its job is done, not just the task of keeping the being that housed it alive—an assignment marked by failure from its very inception—then at least with a sense of what that specific function means. And by now it has gone off to save someone with better possibilities, doubtlessly carrying with it an unfamiliar feeling of peace, and even a certain anxiousness for the story to end once and for all, for all expectations to cease, for the effort to end, for the oh-so-slow bullet to arrive at last. The eternity of souls is an unbearable idea: an endless awareness, flowing, witnessing history, knowing without limits, that unspeakable horror. Knowing is an act of extreme pain, and infinite knowledge belongs only in the worst circle of hell. Then death becomes the only freedom possible.

This is what the observers would have replied, if anybody had asked for their opinion, as Álvaro advanced painfully toward the corner, an objective so humble that it was moving to watch. It wasn't so pretentious, after all: taking that step and going no farther; the corner was a minimal cycle, a stage of starvation, barely a possibility. Even the idea of possibility was remarkable, that there might be something afterward, something that was the orphanage, no doubt, his last refuge, with its mural of the inferno, the dark tower, and the company of Mother Aurora. But getting there was still a premature goal: he had to cover a lot of territory to attain it, one hundred exhausting yards, one hundred terrible lengths of a gorge that stretched before him anguishing, incoherent, overwhelming. At this point, the observers would say that this had gone on beyond all reason. The gesture could be compared to that of the dog who's just been run over by a car; he's lying on his side, he's vomiting blood, his eyes are already cloudy, and yet he wags his tail. Could it be said that this reflects some sort of celebration on the part of the dog? A sign of the life force? Some desire to go on? How does an internal hemorrhage spilling out of one's mouth coexist with that unmistakable gesture of joy? And what should we say then about the nearly undetectable change in Álvaro's attitude, as he now picks up his pace? Ignoring the distance between him and the corner, he arrived sooner than everyone had imagined just a moment before. Were we to think he still harbored some sort of hope, that the famous survival instinct hadn't abandoned him, that in spite of everything, he was still standing, ко'd and all, and in truth what was being inflicted was a definitive coup de grâce, a cross to the jaw—to continue the boxing metaphor that had lodged in Álvaro's brain—or a shot to the back of the head, to borrow the hunter's vocabulary, appropriate for that town of warriors, a merciful gesture on the part of the unconquered champion that could put an end to that heartbreaking agony? As men of faith, the observers believed that if Álvaro still persisted with this attitude, it was because that business had already gone on for longer than was advisable. The best thing was to let him go (if, in fact, he was going to get anywhere, for surely the orphanage was that place, with its infernal mural, its dark tower, and the aforementioned Mother Aurora) and keep waiting, for patience is the hunter's greatest virtue. There would be time later to finish off that tormented man and declare the whole sad story over. One thing was certain: there was no way they would enjoy the outcome; the defeat of a fighter is no cause for celebration. He must be honored and given a Christian burial.

And remain forever in the survivors' memory.

3) TO SEE AND TO DECIDE

He reached the green door and knocked. While he was waiting,

Álvaro looked over his shoulder, but there was no one behind him, and the nuns didn't come running to let him in, either, so he called out, banged on the door, then tried the doorknob, and the door swung open. Inside, the orphans were playing. He made his way among them, greeted them, and moved through what was by now familiar territory, the only thing familiar in that town. He didn't see as many nuns as usual, which struck him as unusual, but he didn't feel up to worrying about other people's affairs. He walked toward the mural of the inferno, always under Christ's stubborn gaze, casually noted the beggar, who felt like an old friend, stopped before the large wooden door, knocked twice, and Aurora's voice—that sanctuary—invited him in.

"You should lock yourself in the tower and wait; time's up now. It's still possible they may not want to come in here. You've seen it yourself—up to now they've just come as far as the door. They could get in: actually, the outer door isn't locked, and nobody will stop them because it's not a matter of force, but it's possible they'll consider the matter over. You and your wife have been a mere accident, and if Dupree has the tapes, you're done for already," said Aurora after listening to Álvaro's tale.

"I still have one copy. Casero had two, and I kept the original," Álvaro muttered, glancing at his Nike Airs. They looked sad.

"And what could you do to them? You don't seem like a great negotiator."

"The tape's in bad condition. I could try to record something else, look for more details, go to the desert… It's still early; I might find something worthwhile. I could pretend to leave town, drive off in the car and come back later. I can't leave just like that. My wife is around here someplace; she might still be alive. Help me, Mother; I can't leave her here without fighting to the end."

"And what makes you imagine this isn't the end?"

"This will end only when I find Alicia," Álvaro replied. He seemed firm, or perhaps stubborn.

"Or when they kill you. They're not stupid. They won't believe that charade. If you leave, don't come back. They'll be tailing you. Follow me," Aurora said, and she blew into the pneumatic tube, facing the back of the room. There, behind a curtain, was a low, dimly lit corridor that veered to the right. Mother Aurora entered and kept moving, with Álvaro following closely behind her. The nun seemed to have more lung power than he did. The chair rolled to the back of the corridor, where there was a door.

"Open it," she said.

Álvaro opened the door, and they entered a small, windowless room, furnished with a chair and a cot. On the cot a pupil was resting.

"This is Patricio Dupree. You're the only one who knows he's here. Not even his father knows about this room. The nun who used to live here left today. She was loyal to me; that's why I made her leave. They're all leaving—you probably noticed that. I'm lost, too. If I'm lucky, they'll transfer me to another diocese, but it's not a sure thing. If things turn out a certain way, this boy could be a strong card; I hope you use it wisely. Are you a Christian?"

"Yes."

{XIII}
AGNUS DEI

THAT NIGHT IN the tower, Álvaro put away his weapons: he left the camera connected, charging his batteries; he checked the videos he had left to use; he hesitated over whether he should erase the takes for his next film till he decided that he was still thinking foolishly. The only video he wasn't going to touch held the images of his wife up to the end. The rest were disposable. If they hunted him down, nothing was going to matter to him anymore, so it was all clear. From the window he watched the patio grow dark; as the sun set and the light faded, the clusters of Mother Aurora's kids thinned out of their own accord and disappeared into their rooms, which was strange to see. The stony-faced nuns hardly circulated now, and order was maintained without any need for guards.

Mother Aurora had insisted that he wait in the tower while she remained in her eternally dark reception room, staring out the window and observing the same view he was seeing at that moment. Álvaro gazed up at Huemul I and noticed that one light was still on: they hadn't even had the decency to turn it off when they fell upon Casero. Someone would come soon to take possession of the place and would take care of all that: paying the electric bill was nothing considering their free use of that office. He felt himself fill up with spite and suddenly felt a strange compulsion to run over there and turn off that light. How far was it? Two blocks, at most. What would be so unusual about going out for a walk at sunset? He was tired of playing Phillip Marlowe; what was this business about—looking for his wife, playing the tough guy? He tormented himself. The result was right before his eyes. He was no good at negotiating, Mother Aurora had said, and it was true: he was a complete failure, useless. He hadn't done anything right. Not even the tape he was hanging onto was of any use, and besides, that fantasy about processing it to improve the image was a real pipedream because, to be frank—and it was hard for him to think this way, like taking a step in the dark, trembling, not knowing if he was about to step on solid ground or into the void—he'd held on to it because deep down he still hoped to return home and tell the story, an awful way to make a name as a film director. He felt like a scumbag; his embarrassment grew like an accusing scarecrow. It was true: he had allowed himself to be carried away by the paltriest of fantasies, but he also knew something else: if all that happened had never spread beyond the town, if no one had come around asking questions, then any accusation, especially with a poor quality, shadowy tape, would end up in the trash can. Or had he really believed that showing the blurry face of a spongy fat guy driving an unrecognizable car was enough to set that madness in motion? Truth was, Casero was already lost to morphine; he was playing a ridiculous card, and what he was trying to do was an act of revenge. They had let him fall, and his only desire had been for them to let him return to the Dupree paradise; all the rest was pure speculation. Regardless, the lawyer hadn't deserved an end like that, or, for that matter, a posthumous, ridiculous homage, but Álvaro didn't know how to do things right; he lived in a celluloid world and saw life the way people went to the movies—in his padded seat, eating popcorn.

He decided to go over and turn off the light.

He went downstairs to the empty patio, crossed it without detecting any signs of movement, half-closed the green metal door, and left. The street was empty; the orphanage punctually reproduced the rhythm of Las Casas. Soon they would come for the children, and the city would once more be a forbidden zone. He walked toward the center of town, trying to keep to the empty lots, rejoicing because his sneakers didn't make noise, just like when he was a boy. He felt almost happy, felt like humming. It was the sweet unconsciousness in which he had lived before; this wasn't a movie, but it was the only thing he knew how to do—to be a harmless idiot who amused himself with his own inventions. An artist, that's what he was, and the truth was that artists didn't bother anybody; they just dedicated their lives to pursuing the crazy dream of feeding a joyful hole that demanded new ideas. If anyone found that offensive, it didn't mean the artist was dangerous (though maybe his creations were), and it was questionable to claim that the one who did those things was responsible for them. An artist produced because of a mandate that was greater than himself; he was merely an instrument, a mentally defective person playing ring around the rosie on the patio of the orphanage. He walked along, loving those kids; he felt closer to Mother Aurora than ever.

He arrived at the building and mounted the five flights of stairs, panting and swearing to give up cigarettes when this misfortune was over. He walked into the office, where he encountered Romano, who was sitting in Casero's chair, rummaging through the desk drawers.

"Aha! The movie hero has arrived. How're you doing, kid? I knew you'd show up here. I don't know why I didn't take Tanco's bet. He was sure you'd go back home today, and I told him no, that kid's hard-headed. I'm a fool, I didn't have faith in myself," he explained, smiling, by way of welcome.

"Bet? What are you talking about? Even I didn't know I was coming here," Álvaro said, disconcerted.

"I wasn't born yesterday, you know. And you had to have some unfinished business here; it was predictable. Even if it was just to turn off the light. No, that was a joke—don't take offense. But you must've had some reason for coming, and even though

I'm not altogether sure what it is, I can imagine. After all, you saw the tapes at Dupree's place, but not their content. I figure there was no VCR available there. Am I wrong?"

"Please go on."

"We took one of Casero's copies, just one, but there's gotta be another. The guy wasn't such a dick that he'd store all his capital in one place. He kept his valuables in the bank, but he was a live wire—while he was alive, of course—and nobody knows the number of his safety deposit box. It's not that hard to find out, but it takes time, and the truth is, Dupree played poker with you. All he wants is for you to leave town and stop breaking his balls. Later, when everything's back to normal, you'll have time to find that tape."

"And you? What do you want?"

"I figure he's gotta have given you the number of his account, as a way to safeguard the merchandise against possible acts of God," said Roman, adding: "You still have a card left to play. You can bluff a little; I can help you."

"You handed over Casero?"

"Why do you say that?"

"Yeah, it was you. That explains why we're talking here. I'm a pariah. I'm almost dead and now you want to help me. You're not such a good person, Romano: either you want a little slice or else you're about to kill me altogether."

"The man's starting to distrust me." Romano looked him straight in the eye and said: "The truth is, I could take you out into the countryside right now, plug you one, and get home in time for dinner. It's obvious that Charlie was the one who talked, and I'll tell you something else: I'll bet my boots he made his own copy while you were waiting at the vault. Never trust Pharisees, bro. The only thing I want is to lend you a hand; it's always healthier for someone to get help from a member of the same club, if you get my drift. And if we make a deal, where's the sin in that? Who knows? I might be turning into a good guy; after all that yakking about piety and loving your neighbor."

"Where's my wife, Romano?"

"I don't know. I swear by my kids," the other man replied with an angelic gesture.

"Why did she go to the hospital that night?"

"She was injured; a bullet grazed her. Nothing serious, don't worry."

"By Mainieri."

"Aha. Now you're starting to catch on."

"What happened after that?"

"Tanco drove her."

"Where to?"

"I don't know that, either. In Las Casas there are questions you shouldn't ask."

"Did she go with Mainieri?"

"Very good. Second deduction confirmed. But Mainieri split and left him alone with her."

"And then?"

"She wasn't seen again. But don't worry—Tanco's the boss around here; he's the second in line after Dupree, and no one touches him. I'm a grunt; I'm just good for running errands."

"He raped her," Álvaro asked or confirmed, trembling.

"It could be: he sure wanted to, and your wife turned out to be very tough. You should've seen how she kicked that old motherfucker in the balls," said Romano, laughing.

Álvaro's heart crumpled. He loved Alicia with all his soul and felt proud of her. Two tears rolled out of his eyes, and he turned his head toward the window: from there he could see the patio of the orphanage, a little box, glowing white beneath the waxing moon. Behind it was the dark tower where his camera batteries were charging. He spied the black car circulating along the street where the orphanage stood; the car was idling, with a direct view of the green door. The dark outlines of some men emerged from the car. This time they walked through the green door. More silhouettes entered, dispersed, and after a while came out of the building with several children. In the white glow of the moonlight he thought he saw someone pushing a wheelchair. This was turning into a major event. The Huemulenses' favorite sport was about to begin.

"What do they call people who were born in Los Huemules?"

"Huemules, that's what they call us. Not Huemulenses or Huemulinos, please. We're Huemules. That's the way it's always been, from the beginning."

"Yes, and you're also disappearing, I've noticed," Álvaro continued, distracted by the scene he was viewing like a mockup. There was a tiny movement down below on the patio, and though it was hard to make out the faces, it wasn't really necessary: now the nuns were exiting through the green door, their faces hidden.

"Don't you believe it—we're tough, and God is a huemul. Look, kid, I'm going to offer you a deal. You go to the bank and make the copy. I'll pretend not to know what's going on and cover your tracks. We'll meet at Arizmendi's place and we'll sell the tape to the TV station. The way the world is now, in a couple of days it'll even be on CNN. We can make enough cash to live comfortably for the rest of our lives. We can even make your movie."

There was a silence. Álvaro kept staring out the window; he looked at Dupree's point man and pulled out the slip of paper with the account number.

"Here's what I think of your deal, motherfucker," Álvaro said, showing him the slip of paper before he swallowed it.

Romano was speechless. He didn't get up, he didn't make a move, and he didn't say a word. When Álvaro left the office, he heard the point man's frantic voice reaching him from the upper floors:

"Maybe you should hide in your mother's cunt, asshole, 'cause if I ever see you around here, I'll beat the shit out of you. And you know what? I'm the one who fucked your wife, you hear me? All week long I fucked her up the ass, and two hours ago I put a bullet into the back of her head. Did you hear that, faggot? And watch out: you're living on borrowed time."

He ran downstairs, stunned, frantic, terrified that Romano would pursue him; he had nothing to defend himself with. And yet he kept on going until he reached the exit. The point man was in no hurry; he could hunt him down today or tomorrow; he had all the time and power in the universe. Álvaro stopped beside the door, waiting. After a while he heard measured footsteps; the man was walking along, whistling. He saw him pass by and allowed him to take one more step, till he was right in front of him, and then he grabbed him by the neck. He knocked him onto his back, punched him in the face and kept on punching. Romano didn't seem to understand where the blows were coming from and didn't try to defend himself. Álvaro kept on hitting; he climbed up on top of the other man's belly, grabbed him by the ears, and started banging his head against the curb. He saw Romano's expression of surprise and fright, enjoying it like a savage; he saw his closed eyes and his gaping, silent mouth; he grew more and more excited to hurt and defeat his enemy. Álvaro was killing him and he wouldn't stop; this was no deliberate act of will that delivered the punishment: something brutal and uncontrollable was propelling him along. He punched and yanked and pulled, not paying much attention to what was tangled between his fingers. It was a strange, silent battle, with only one contender. The fallen man never understood what was happening, nor did he put up any resistance. Álvaro didn't speak or scream; it was all an angry groan that accompanied his movements. He felt the point man's body buck under his legs and he kept on punching. He discharged all the blows that his body ordered, hitting and hitting till Romano lay still. Then he got up, soaked in the criminal's blood, nearly out of breath, confused, and exhausted. He looked around, but all the windows were closed, as they were supposed to be. He frisked Romano, took his revolver, and stuck it in his waistband. Then he grabbed him by the shoulders and dragged him into the building, opened the elevator's accordion door, and dropped the body down the shaft. It was a couple of yards, at most, to the bottom, not counting the security springs and the piled-up trash. When Romano hit bottom, Álvaro heard a moan. He was surprised. He sharpened his hearing and noticed a hissing sound—death rales, perhaps? He closed the door and left.

{XIV}
LUX AETERNA

THE ORPHANAGE seemed empty. Álvaro ran to the room in the tower, which was still dark and untouched, picked up his camera and Alicia's little bag, went down to the patio, then to Mother Aurora's room, but the nun was no longer there. He wasn't going to find out anything; the die had already been cast. He passed through the curtain in back, went to Patricio's room and woke him. The boy was startled by the unfamiliar, bloody man.

"Hi, Patricio"—he showed him the camera—"I'm from the TV station. Would you like to be on TV?"

Álvaro turned on the camera and looked at him through the viewer. The boy smiled and allowed himself to be photographed. He purred with pleasure.

"What's your name?" Álvaro asked, with the camera running.

"My name is Patricio. What's yours?" Patricio's face was illuminated.

"My name is Álvaro. I want you to come downstairs to the street. with me. Today we're going to make a movie. Would you like to do that?"

"Let's go! Is it about outer space? Is it *Star Wars*? Is R2D2 here?" asked the elated boy, whose head was broad in front and flattened on the sides. He didn't seem seriously disabled.

"No, it's about shooting, but don't be scared because I'll take care of you."

When they left the building, some explosions could already be heard at the dark, far end of the avenue, where Dupree's estancia was. There was no visible movement nearby, and they walked easily to the car, which was parked half a block away. Álvaro sat Patricio next to him, fastened the boy's seat belt, checked to make sure the windows were closed and the doors locked, readied the camera, turned on the light inside the car, turned on the high beams, revved the motor, and headed toward the noise. The coupe was a dream; the engine was almost inaudible. They came to an intersection, and when they could hear sounds, he started to film. Like in a vaudeville scene, two little girls ran past the headlights, hand in hand, in their white nightgowns, one of them dark-haired, the other blonder; at that distance it was impossible to tell their condition; they looked more like a dream than a nightmare. A moment later, when the girls were out of the headlights' beam, but with their glowing nightgowns still revealing which shrubs they were hiding in, the dogs whizzed past the coupe like arrows. At the same time, a shot rang out from right to left, though outside the frame, where the little girls had already been cornered by the mastiffs. Then came another, identical gunshot, which the camera picked up, implacably. Patricio groaned, and Álvaro took his hand. Then Mainieri entered the frame from the right; he was armed with a shotgun and fired for the third time, and for the third time his shot was captured by the camera, now with his image at the exact moment when he first noticed the light, and then Álvaro inside the car. The camera picked up the details of Mainieri's expression, which went from surprise, when he saw Álvaro, to fury, when he turned toward him, raised his weapon, aimed, and walked toward the car. There was a zoom and an extreme close-up of the weapon, and behind that, on opening the lens, Mainieri's astonished face, his threatening gestures. Something said this wouldn't be understandable, though it was clear what it all was about. Patricio grew agitated.

"Relax, they won't hurt you," Álvaro soothed him and pulled out Romano's revolver. Mainieri took a few steps and stopped. He leaned over a little, without lowering his gun, and he recognized Patricio. His eyes opened wide with alarm as he looked at Álvaro, who was aiming the revolver at the boy's temple; then he looked at Patricio again. Álvaro was still filming when Mainieri bent over; he caught Mainieri's astonished expression on seeing who the hostage was, captured the moment when Mainieri lowered his gun and when he turned around and when he ran away toward the dark foliage.

"Is it over?" Patricio asked. He was terrified.

"Not yet. Come with me." Álvaro put the weapon away.

They got out of the car, ran to the corner, and hid behind a partially destroyed wall that faced a vacant lot.

"Nice and quiet now, Patricio. Soon some men with guns are going to come. They won't see us, but we'll see them, and we're going to tape it all for TV, okay?"

"What's happening?"

"It looks as if they're hunting your friends from the Home, but it's only a movie, nothing more. See? Look over there."

Álvaro took an 80-meter zoom and focused on Ayala, who appeared beneath the moonlight, crossed by the coupe's headlights. He was ghostly image, fierce and obese, accompanied by three other men: the Chief of Police was dragging a little child, bleating and struggling, by the hair. Álvaro understood that he and Mainieri had lost contact which gave him a little more time. The child continued to struggle; they dragged him and he shrieked, kicked, and groped until the Chief pulled his revolver from the holster, pressed it against the boy's temple, and pulled the trigger: the camera captured the head exploding and the blood spattering against his face and shirt.

"Is it real?" Patrick asked, crying.

"Quiet now," Álvaro ordered. Patrick swallowed his tears and his snot.

More men showed up and converged around Ayala, who was now concentrating, astonished, on Álvaro's Chevy. Just then Mainieri arrived, dazed, devoid of plans. He walked over to the chief and started to talk to him, pointing to the car, and the chief, barely listening, trampled on the clerk's words; he asked, he interrupted, he made faces, and Mainieri offered explanations, lots of them, everything the chief asked for, and as he explained again and again, he gestured, pointing out what had happened in the car; Ayala's expression changed; the man couldn't believe what he was hearing; he shook the clerk, he poked his chest with a stiff index finger, the finger drummed him below his police shield, it distressed him, it made him pull back while the chief asked and repeated the question; then he insulted him and looked at the other men; trying to corroborate Mainieri's lame explanations, but the men's faces were blank and servile. Then the flabby body straightened up and now looked like a depraved soldier, bizarre and fat-assed; now he was the very depiction of anxiety, because at last he understood that the priest's son had been seen with Álvaro. His face was a perfect portrait of fear and rage, of a broken guarantee. The chief turned away from Mainieri, and the men sprung into motion; fearfully and slowly, they approached the coupe; with their readied weapons and tense flashlights, they arrived, checked the car, and immediately abandoned the search and began to discuss something. Then Ayala rebuked Mainieri, who took another step backward while the men looked all around. The flashlights came and went, spun and turned in the tight shadows. They tried to see, but their lights were few and the search, unlikely. Finally, the chief gave a sign and everyone left.

"Let's go, Patricio, come with me."

Álvaro took the boy by the hand and they ran toward the car: again the seat belt, the locks, windows closed. Then Álvaro turned the motor over, made a U-turn and headed toward the exit from town. The tires squealed, the engine roared, and the men returned. A bullet whistled high above, then two more on either side; one rebounded off the roof and rose up in the air; another blew off the right rear-view mirror. Álvaro just sped up and prayed the tires would hold. He ran two blinking red lights on the avenue. The square was behind him, on his left, he vaguely realized; for one second, El Tolo's garage was on his right. Then he passed Fabiana's pensión; two blocks farther he crossed—as if in a nightmare—opposite the Seagull. Sensing red lights ahead, he hit the gas, took the curve, and found himself on the road to the garbage dump.

The men were coming, time was running out, they had to escape, only escape, nothing more than that. He accelerated and gained distance; they were leaving; the hunters had been left behind. But then he slammed on the brakes.

In front of the car were the wild dogs.

If Álvaro had imagined a few nasty scavenger dogs prowling around the outskirts of town, the thing that now blocked his way assumed the scale of a horrible dream: There must have been around a hundred dogs, he quickly calculated, but there might as well have been a hundred thousand, and maybe there really were; it was impossible to know. Stunned and vaguely fascinated, he found himself in the presence of a deranged demonstration of power in which their eyes, glowing in his headlights, barely outlined the borders of the pack. Without taking his eyes off them, Álvaro groped the dashboard until he managed to turn off the lights; only then did he behold a colossal mass of brown silhouettes before him, tangled and alert, barely illuminated by the moon, a single, incalculable beast that spread out before him, upwards and down along the sides. That brutality of eyes, fangs, and dripping foam gathered together at the intruders' arrival. Álvaro glimpsed an abyss of heads peeking out among crowded spines, an immeasurable legion where formless outlines of tall, pointed ears, ravenous maws and angry snouts could barely be distinguished. The dogs were the undisputed owners of that territory; they had been invaded and there they were, ready to fall upon them. That delirium of eager wild beasts stretched as far as the eye could see, and worse yet, more kept arriving from the desert. Behind them rose a bulldozer, like a sickly pyramid encountered along the way. On the roof of the cab outlined by the light of the moon, stood the enormous, overwhelming black shadow of the leader, vertical and priestly, jealously guarding his pack, his vast ears pointing toward the thrumming of the coupe.

Like one who dreams his most fearsome dream and conjures it by force of habit, Álvaro had taken out his camera and turned it on, perhaps thinking about recording his own death, regretting the inadequate light, all the while taking note of that numberless multitude of predators. At that moment, the sound of engines came from behind, and Álvaro emerged from his daydream, let go of the camera, looked at Patricio and made up his mind: he turned the steering wheel to the right, slammed the gas pedal, and took off like a shot, flattening piles of trash. He rattled along into the garbage dump, getting stuck and unstuck again, advancing aimlessly, accelerating and hearing the engines, first behind him, then to his right, then behind him again, now to the left, ahead of him. He went round and round, finding no way out. He was about to crash into a tall heap of waste when he braked suddenly: the piles of trash rose up like mountains on all sides, preventing him from seeing the headlights of the cars, though they sounded as if they were close by. Between the elevations there were depressions, small, empty spaces where not very distant flat areas seemed likely to be: the way out had to lie in one of them. He had kept his lights off, guiding himself by the moon, in order to keep the men from spotting him, but he decided it was a necessary risk, so he turned them on again.

Anyone watching would have said that she was lying on her back, taking an impossible siesta; her head rested on a bag of trash, turned to one side. She seemed distracted, as if staring at something on the horizon. Her forehead had been bleeding, but those intrepid black curls—so flattened and so damp—hadn't been touched. Half-hidden among scraps of food that spilled over one shoulder, but not the other, with her right leg supported, as if carelessly, by a tire that hid her foot. The left leg, bent in what might have been a ballet position, still wore its sandal. She had fallen face up, more diagonal than horizontal, her arms flung open, one palm up and the other down. She wore her red fisherman's pants, and on her shirt, the name ALICIA was still legible.

Álvaro got out of the car. Patricio saw him walk into the beam of light and approach the apparently resting woman; he saw him embrace and caress her, he saw how he brushed her hair aside and kissed her forehead, pressing her against his chest, and he saw his expression change from pain to outrage, from outrage to despair, from despair to calm. He saw him weep and kiss her again; he saw his head resting on the woman's chest, and he saw her head shaking as if saying yes and then saying no. And he understood that the woman was someone important and that it wasn't a movie.

At that moment, to his left, a light passed across the flat horizon, heading north. Patricio realized that *that* was the road they were looking for.

The wild dogs had followed them; they had already reached the car and were starting to surround it. They moved slowly, cautiously, in silence. Patricio saw the leader of the pack on top of a pile of garbage. That animal kept watch over everything because—it was enough just to see him—he was the god of the dogs. When they were completely surrounded, he saw Álvaro spin around and discover those jaws clamped onto his legs; he saw Álvaro's petrified expression; he saw him step backward and try to climb the heap of trash with his heels digging into the pile; he wished with all his heart that Álvaro would make it; and he despaired at seeing him slip, and knowing that the dogs could climb that hill better than Álvaro could. He also noticed that the dogs hardly moved. He looked at the alpha dog and perceived some connection with that strange calm; he struggled to understand. He saw that the dogs were watching Álvaro carefully and that the leader watched over all of them. It was as if the whole world depended on that terrible beast. He thought that they understood one another in a way he didn't exactly comprehend; now he could see it: the leader was calm, and the others blinked attentively, and if that were to change, if that animal were to get angry, he would give them an order: he would instruct the wild dogs to eat Álvaro and the woman. And him, too, he understood, even if he remained inside the car. The animals repressed their moans, they sniffed, showing their teeth, but they didn't move. Álvaro was getting agitated. Patricio watched his chest pumping, and became frightened when Álvaro suddenly turned his back on them. You would need the bravery of a giant to do that. Then he saw Álvaro kneel and pick up the woman, stand with her in his arms, then turn around again, this time facing the wild dogs head on, and advance two steps; he stopped and deposited her on the ground, placing her right there, anointed, within reach of the dogs. Then he took two steps backward and waited. There was a hesitation, a moment of intense, repressed rage. Álvaro waited, and nothing happened: the dogs remained in place, and he stood, motionless as a statue. Álvaro waited and the dogs waited, until suddenly they seemed to understand. Then there was something like a thunderbolt, a gigantic clamor fell upon the woman's body and filled the air with the sounds of slaughter; there were ravenous outbursts, tugging and furious grunts, threats and angry fangs, an overpowering maelstrom that converged into frenetic spurts, in cries of pain and triumph, of animals that moved toward the center and of others that walked away, rejected and defeated. The scene changed, turning into brief skirmishes along the edges; some expired and bled, and the blood inflamed the rivals that balanced on top of them, unbound in that bestial fury; the largest ones fell on the wounded, and the garbage dump became a war zone, filled with howls of death. Along those same borders, Álvaro advanced, circling the storm of dogs. He avoided that sea of maws, skirting the beasts, taking measured steps, one step and pause, another step and pause again, slowly, slowly, hardly touching the ground, not brushing anything, not moving the air, not existing. The dogs barely noticed him. Some were suspicious and bared their teeth at him, but as he withdrew from the center of the crowd, they ignored his presence, watching him out of the corners of their eyes, sniffing his scent. They growled and struggled among themselves, more interested in fighting their way into the circle where the fiercest among them huddled. Álvaro drew nearer. Patricio saw him coming, as in a dream; he thought Álvaro was smiling; he saw him approach the car, transformed, his eyes fixed on every move he made, trembling. He stopped beside the door: some animals were wandering around near the car and could get in when he opened it. If the door grazed even one of them, it would infuriate the rest of the pack. Sweating, trying to control the trembling of his hand, Álvaro grabbed the door handle and triggered the mechanism. And then the men arrived.

They came from the right; the horizon filled up with long beams of light; cars and vans stopped, lined up, and illuminated the bedlam with powerful headlights. A thousand bristling spines turned like a single jumble of fur and rage, tensed before the invasion; the beasts saw the men descending from the vans, but they didn't move, and then they saw the mastiffs as well. A tremendous roar erupted from above. The hideous colossus stood erect, nearly brushing the moon with its ears; its jaws opened like a bulldozer and it roared again; its howls echoing throughout the desert. It felt like a hurricane was blowing through, and when the pack responded to the call, the world burst into flames. A single beast with a thousand howling faces, like a legion of hellish, aborted fetuses launched a stampede toward the lights, where the mastiffs were barking furiously. The men fired shots and climbed into their vehicles, but the mastiffs remained below. The wild dogs ignored the coupe and ran down to attack them; the place was left deserted. A frenzied chorus of roars broke out, and the mastiffs squealed in pain from the center of the battle, as the engines disappeared on their way back to town, and the seagulls squawked as they flew over the garbage dump. Álvaro got back into the car.

He was shaking, his teeth chattered, and his eyes seemed lost at a distant point on the horizon. He was in the car, but it seemed like he was still standing outside, and he was still shaking when Patricio explained his discovery, telling him where the road was. Gradually he understood and pulled himself together. Stunned, he looked at what the boy was showing him, and he blinked; it felt like he was getting lost again. He looked back at the boy, dazed, and his eyes cleared a little. Once again he turned toward the horizon. Patricio repeated that the road was in that direction, and then, for the last time, he checked the seat belt and the door locks, took the boy by the shoulders, gave him a kiss on the head, said "Let's go," turned over the motor, accelerated with more fear than desire; the car started to move, he turned left, followed the road, passed the last stretch of the garbage dump; the coupe mounted the embankment and landed squarely on the asphalt. Then he stepped on the gas till the speedometer read 90 mph.

After a while, Patricio asked:

"Are you my dad?"

It took Álvaro another sixty miles to reply:

"Yes, Patricio, I'm your dad."

In memory of the 3,000, still waiting

AUTHOR BIO

Writer and Psychiatrist GUSTAVO EDUARDO ABREVAYA was born in Buenos Aires in 1952. His writing has appeared in numerous magazines and anthologies. He is the author of the novels *El criadero*, *Los Infernautas*, and *The Envoy* (with Leonardo Killian). In 2020, he was selected as a permanent juror for the noir novel competition of the Black Mountain Bossost Festival in Bossost, Spain. He is currently working on a series of novels about a war between police officers. *El criadero* was originally published in Argentina, and was subsequently published in Cuba and Spain, where it won the 2002 José Boris Spivacow Award. Appearing here as *The Sanctuary*, it marks Abrevaya's first translation into English.

TRANSLATOR BIO

ANDREA G. LABINGER has published numerous translations of Latin American fiction. *Gesell Dome*, her translation of Guillermo Saccomanno's noir novel *Cámara Gesell* (Open Letter 2016), won a PEN/Heim Translation Award and was long-listed for the Community of Literary Magazines and Presses' Firecracker Award. She also translated Saccomanno's *77* (Open Letter 2019). She previously translated Patricia Ratto's *Proceed With Caution* (2021) for Schaffner Press.